Champagne Witches

A Shot of Midlife Magic Book 1

Tegan Maher

Copyright © 2022 by Tegan Maher

All rights reserved.

No part of this book may be reproduced in any form or by any electronic or mechanical means, including information storage and retrieval systems, without written permission from the author, except for the use of brief quotations in a book review.

Introduction

Hi! Welcome to Champagne Witches, the first book in my A Shot of Midlife Magic paranormal women's fiction series. I thought I'd take a second to tell you about the book and about the motivations behind it.

First off, this isn't a cozy. It's heavier on the romance scenes and does have some swearing, but there's no graphic sex scenes.

As all of my characters do, Jules popped into my imagination fully formed and demanding that I tell her story. Writing about a strong, older character appealed to me, as I'm not getting any younger myself, and it was nice to step away from murder mysteries for a while, too.

On a final note, no parrots were harmed in the writing of this book. Enjoy!

Prologue

Did you ever have one of those days where suck just piles onto more suck until you're positive you're never going to be able to crawl out from under it? My story starts on one of those days. In fact, it was so bad that it created one of those major forks in the road that pushed me out of the old and into the unknown. In hindsight, it was exactly what I needed, but it took me some time, a lot of margaritas, and a major shift in perspective to get there.

First, let's back up for a second so I can give you the backstory before I launch into what I've come to call The Day That Changed Everything. After all, I'm still just a random stranger to you, and there's nothing worse than some nutjob middle-aged chick dumping her drama on you out of the blue.

My name is Jules Cavanaugh, and before The Day, I was your stereotypical middle-aged soccer mom of two turned empty-nester. I spent most of my life running myself ragged getting the kids from one extracurricular activity to the next, which I took extreme pleasure in doing. I was also the perfect executive's wife, hosting fancy business dinners and having the perfunctory vanilla sex once weekly. That part was a drag.

I wasn't born to be a stuffy member of the upper crust, and my husband hadn't been like that when I met him. Back then, he'd been a free spirit, but his ladder-climbing drive to be the best got the better of him, and me by association. Our marriage, which had started with us lying awake at night in our little studio apartment dreaming of how far we were going to go, was collateral damage to ambition and the corporate machine.

My two best friends, CiCi and Laurel, were my saviors through the years. We met in college and formed a posse that had withstood two decades of sick kids, birthday parties, and PTA drama. They were always ready to follow stuffy Friday night dinners with Saturday morning mimosa brunches. Since we were rowing the same boat together, it was a much-needed way to blow off steam.

Cici was a tall, curvy brunette who still wore the same size she had in high school. Laurel was a bit more like me. We'd both developed an allergy to spin class at the same time our metabolisms had turned to molasses. We hadn't let ourselves completely go, but we both had a bit more junk in the trunk than was strictly necessary. Thankfully, none of us were dealing with full-on menopause yet, but the hot flashes, moodiness, and stray chin hairs were popping up here and there to give us a glimpse of the not-so-glorious things to come.

That's all just side story, though. The important part is that I owe my new and improved existence to them. They're the ones who booted me toward greener pastures even while I was grasping for the smoky yet safe remnants of life as I'd known it. Some things just can't be fixed, and they saw that sooner than I did.

That brings us to my origin story, so to speak. The Day That Changed Everything.

Chapter One

The Day was a Monday because ... of course it was. I'd dropped my youngest son, Bryan, off at Penn State the day before, opting to drive him rather than put him on a plane in order to milk as much time with him as possible before he was officially a grownup and I was an empty nester.

It was worse for me with him than it had been with my oldest son, Derek, because Bryan was the one most like me. While Derek was business-minded and serious like his father, Bryan was the dreamer. Derek never cracked a higher math book to keep his perfect GPA, and Bryan, like me, struggled with basic algebra while excelling in language and arts. They were as close as two brothers could be, but they surely were two very different peas sharing a pod.

Anyway, I'd arrived home to an empty house, which wasn't unusual. I was sort of glad, actually, because I was still an emotional mess even after crying for most of the long drive home. I'd taken a shower and gone to bed in Bryan's room. Yeah, pathetic and a little weird, I know, but it was what my heart needed at the time.

Rob was already gone to work when I got up the next morning, so I went about my daily errands. Grocery shopping for two was an adjustment, but I managed to make it through, even though the decided lack of junk food was a glaring reminder that my babies were gone.

At the last minute, I whipped into the local community college. I had an art degree I'd never done much with, but art history was more than just something I learned about in college and forgot—it was a life-long passion and one that I figured I might enjoy passing on. With the kids gone, I was going to need something to fill my days, and I enjoyed teaching.

On a whim, I popped into Victoria's Secret and picked up a black number that would highlight the ladies and downplay the soggy middle. Now that we could run naked in the house, it was time to spice things up a bit.

With a head full of lascivious thoughts, I was awash with confidence as I drove up our street. That dimmed a bit when I caught sight of a shiny red Porsche outside.

I did my best to shrug off the disappointment. It was probably one of Rob's work buddies stopping by for a drink while they talked shop, so he wouldn't be there long. We'd waited twenty years to have the house to ourselves. Another hour wouldn't make a difference.

I grabbed the two piddly bags of groceries from the back of my minivan and stuffed the see-through lingerie bag in with the dried goods, smiling when I pictured the look on his face. We used to have intense chemistry, and I was looking forward to getting that spark back.

Plopping the groceries down on the marble island that had groaned under the weight of a thousand business-function appetizers and family holiday meals, I peered into the den to see who was here and was a little surprised to find it empty.

"Rob?" I called. "Where are you guys? Do you need anything while I'm in here?"

"We're in the sitting room, Juliette."

I arched a brow. He hadn't called me Juliette since we took our vows. The whole, "Do you, Robert, take Juliette" part. In fact, nobody called me that. That and the weight in his voice were the first whiffs I had of the bullshit to come. I made my way toward the living room, each step measured.

At first, what I saw didn't make any sense.

Robert and Bubbles, our secretary—yes, her actual given name was Rainbow Bubbles thanks to obviously stoned parents—sat close together on the cream linen sofa. His hands were folded in his lap, and her hand was on his thigh.

"What the hell's going on here?" I asked, my gaze bouncing back and forth between them.

He had the grace to look away, but she sat straighter and thrust her chin—and by default her disgustingly perky boobs—out, defiant. I narrowed my eyes at them, understanding creeping in. I'm a lot of things, but stupid isn't one of them. Apparently, I had to fess up to being gullible, though. All those late nights and weekends suddenly made much more sense.

My brain disconnected from my emotions, leaving nothing but a disjointed clarity. Somewhere in the back of my mind, I knew that wouldn't last, but I prayed to whatever powers were out there that I could maintain it until I could get them out of the house. "How long has this been going on?"

Subdued, Rob replied, "Almost a year."

"Huh," I said, nodding as I tried to process whatever

this was. "And why are you bringing it up now? And why is she here?"

Our voices sounded like they were coming through a tunnel, tinny and far away, but I could hear every word with crystal clarity.

He pulled in a deep sigh. "I didn't want to hit you with it yesterday when you were upset about dropping Bryan off at school—"

Before he could finish, she cut in. "We're in love and gettin' married."

My gaze whipped to her, and the shocked calm that had settled over me minutes before burned up like mist, leaving nothing but white-hot rage. "There's only one problem with that, little girl. He's already married."

I don't know what made me say that because of course, they were here to tell me Rob wanted a divorce. Maybe I just wanted to drive home the fact that she was a homewrecker. I shook my head. That wasn't right. *He* was a homewrecker. As smug as that little bitch was, she had no obligation to me. We hadn't said any vows or made any promises, and I was all for putting the blame directly where it belonged.

I held my hand up, shutting her down, and turned to Rob. "Excuse me, but did you say you didn't want to tell me yesterday because you knew I was upset about Bryan? And you thought that would just go away today, so trotting Miss Twinkle Tits in here would be just fine and dandy? Bless your heart, and get the hell out of my house."

Had I been able to shoot fire from my eyes, there'd be nothing left of them but two scorched spots on my sofa.

Rob held up a finger. "About the house—"

"Out!" I jammed my finger toward the door, then pulled it back before he could see how badly it was shaking. I had about ten seconds before I either broke down into a crying mess or fetched my memaw's iron skillet and beat the rotten cheater to death with it. I didn't think he needed to be around to see which side that quarter landed on.

Unlike my dunce of a husband, Bubbles recognized the expression on my face for what it was—impending doom— and beat it toward the door, barely pausing to snatch her Louis Vuitton purse from the couch.

He opened his mouth and closed it again, then turned on his heel and slunk out, pulling the door shut behind him. I made my way to the picture window and peeked out the mauve crushed-velvet drapes just to make sure they actually left, then sank into the nearest chair to process what had just happened.

The more I thought about it, the madder I got, which was a good thing. The only three logical options were rage, grief, and self-pity, and the latter two had no place in this situation. They'd come, sure, but for that moment, I was content to let my temper rule the day.

I won't regale you with the glorious tantrum I threw, but suffice it to say that a Southern woman scorned is a sight to behold. Once my anger had run its course, the self-pity took hold, and I made a conference call to my two besties. True to form, they were at my house in less than ten minutes, Laurel toting a bottle of the good tequila and CiCi trailing behind with a bag of limes.

They took one look at me and rushed forward, pulling me into their arms.

CiCi rubbed my back as I struggled to hold it together. "Baby girl, don't swallow the storm. Let it out."

That was all it took—the dam broke, and all the hurt and anger and sense of betrayal poured out. They hugged me and let me cry like my heart was breaking into a thousand pieces, because it was as surely as my marriage had.

After a few minutes, I drew in a deep, shaky breath and swallowed, then swiped at my face. Unlike all the Southern belles on TV, I was an ugly crier. I had no doubt my eyes were red and puffy, my mascara was running down my face, and my nose was running like a sugar tree. I tried to laugh through my tears because that's what this situation was— laugh or cry, and I was done cryin'.

"Holy shit." Laurel glanced around the living room in awe, taking in the disaster of broken vases, busted wedding pictures, and the golf club still sticking out of the big screen. "It looks like we're drinkin' in the kitchen."

I smiled at that despite the situation, just grateful for the lack of judgment.

"So what are you gonna do?" CiCi asked once we'd left the tornado of rage-induced destruction behind and settled down at the white wicker table in the breakfast nook.

I slammed the shot of tequila Laurel handed me, then winced as I bit into the lime wedge. "What *can* I do? It's not like he bounced a check or wrecked the car. He cheated on me with a twenty-something twit named Bubbles, for Christ's sake. What I'm gonna do is get blind-drunk with you two. Whatever I do next will have to wait until tomorrow."

Laurel, being the wise soul she is, decided we'd do better with margaritas to sip rather than straight tequila that went down smooth as butter. Three frozen concoctions and several rounds of cursing and poxing later, we ran out of things to call him. Content that a fly wouldn't light on him even if he were covered in honey, I sighed, then hiccuped.

"What am I gonna do, guys?" I studied the last tiny bit of melted green liquid pooling in the bottom of my glass like it held the secrets to the universe. "I have no job, no money, and nowhere to go. If he decides to sell the house, I'm screwed. I've done nothing but sign the checks for the business for the last twenty years."

It was a defeatist attitude, but after the day I'd had, I figured a little wallowing was acceptable.

CiCi's brunette brow popped up. "You may not have a job, but you have half his money plus alimony if you get a good lawyer. As for the house, do you really want to stay here anyway? I mean, when I got divorced, everything in the place reminded me either of the good times, which depressed the crap out of me, or the bad times, which infuriated me."

Laurel bobbed her head, sending her champagne curls wobbling. She squinted one eye, probably to see me through the tequila goggles, then jerked her thumb toward CiCi. "I'm with her. You don't wanna stay here. Maybe if the boys were still around, but you'll have constant reminders that they're gone too, and you were already struggling with that before your piece-of-shit husband dropped his bomb. It's better to let it go and get another place. Start fresh."

I rose and made another round of margaritas, my mind whirling as fast as the blender blades despite the copious amounts of alcohol saturating it. "If I had half a brain, I'd pack my crap and move to my dad's place in Florida. Seeya, Rob and Bubbles." I flapped my hand, then grasped the counter when the exaggerated movement knocked me off balance. "The boys can visit me anywhere now, and I'm sick of the cold anyway. Besides, I don't wanna be the one everybody gets all pity-eyed at whenever I run into them in the grocery store."

My father had passed away a month or so before, and I hadn't had a chance to deal with his estate yet. He'd left when I was ten, and we hadn't been close, so all I really knew was that he'd owned some sort of bar on Florida's Gulf Coast and left it to me.

When I turned off the blender, it took a minute for my pickled brain to realize that my chatty friends had gone silent. When I turned to them, they were staring at me. CiCi had her hand over her mouth, and Laurel was nodding.

I struggled to think what I might have said to strike them speechless since I'd never managed it before. Or maybe I had lime on my face. I scrubbed a hand over it, but nada. I scowled at them. "What? Have I sprouted a giant zit?"

They looked at each other, and matching Cheshire-Cat grins spread across their faces. CiCi spoke first. "That's exactly what you're gonna do. You're movin' to Florida."

Chapter Two

I woke up the next morning surprisingly un-hungover. We'd spent half the night going through my clothes, and there was now a huge pile of expensive but boring clothes "appropriate" for the middle-aged wife of an important executive. There were a few ball gowns in the pile too.

What was left was one small suitcase of casual clothes and one garment bag containing three flirty cocktail dresses with matching shoes and clutches that had been in the back of the closet left over from the early days.

I pulled in a deep breath, questioning my sanity. The idea of a fresh start surrounded by sun, sand, and fruity cocktails had seemed magical last night, but now my common sense was kicking in. No good decision was ever made between midnight and sunrise.

My phone rang, and I scrambled to grab it from the nightstand. It was a group call from my two partners in crime.

"You're thinking about backing out," CiCi said, and I could practically see her green eyes narrowing.

"Don't even think about it," Laurel admonished. "In fact, come open the front door."

Still holding the phone to my ear, I did as she said. There they both stood, Laurel holding a cardboard carrier with three venti coffees and CiCi clutching three huge shopping bags.

I blinked, still trying to clear the sleep—and remnants of tequila—from my brain. "What's all that?"

"This," CiCi replied as she pushed past me, "is some stuff to fill in the grotesque gaps in your new wardrobe. You can't show up down there in ratty mom jeans and yuppie button-down shirts. You're starting a new life, for god's sake, and you're not dragging Rob with you even if it is only in the form of frumpy clothes."

I took the coffee CiCi handed me and peered into the closest bag. Bright T-shirts, tank tops, and hoodies created a kaleidoscope of color.

I pulled out a pretty Kona-blue V-neck sleeveless blouse and held it up in front of me, then set it aside and pilfered through the bag for the next—a green tank top with a gold pocket. "There must be twenty shirts in here."

CiCi smiled. "Eighteen. I remember you in college. One basket for clean clothes and one for dirty, and you didn't do laundry until the clean one was empty. Besides, we don't know if you'll have a washer and dryer there, and we'd rather not have you brutally murdered in a laundromat."

I laughed, feeling a little lightheaded as I tried to wrap my mind around the fact that I would no longer be responsible for ironing dress shirts, getting the stains out of football jerseys, or mating mountains of socks.

I took a gulp of coffee to fight back the panic. That's all I'd done for the last twenty years. To give my brain something else to focus on, I reached for the next bag and pulled out a tangled mess of strappy sandals and flip-flops.

"It's the official footwear of Florida," Cici said, reaching over to help me untangle them. "We picked some cute ones to go with what's in the next bag, and a few pairs to wear every day or to the beach."

The third bag had several cute sundresses and several pairs of shorts in fabrics ranging from denim to linen. I reached to the bottom and pulled out a pair of jeans, then laughed when I saw the low waist and casual, stylish rips in them.

"Remember when we used to have to wear them forever to get that look? Now they charge extra for it." Laurel smiled, then sniffed. "I swore I wasn't going to cry, but I'm gonna miss you hard, girl."

I leaned over and scooped her into a hug, and CiCi joined us. These women had been with me through good times and bad, and my resolve to leave began to melt. I couldn't imagine starting over in a strange place without them.

CiCi pushed back from me and wagged one finger while carefully wiping a tear from her eye without mussing her makeup. "Flights are cheap, and it's a short flight from here to Dolphin Key. We'll see each other all the time. And we're not payin' for our drinks when we come, either."

I smiled through my tears. "Are you kidding? Drinks on the house whenever you visit!"

I had no idea what condition, financial or otherwise, the bar was in, but if there was a bottle of tequila, then it was ready and waiting whenever they decided to come.

The silence stretched, and it got to the point that I was making excuses not to leave, but it was time.

"Did you tell Rob yet?" Laurel asked.

I stood from the breakfast nook and gave her a wicked grin. "I laid awake for an hour last night trying to figure out how I was gonna tell him. I decided to go with this."

I held up an envelope, and both of them squealed with laughter as they stepped closer and read it.

"It's perfect!" they chimed.

I'd simply plucked the nearest bill out of the mail basket and written "Moved to Florida" on the back of it.

I shrugged. "I suppose he'll find it when he stops to get his things."

I knew I'd have to deal with him in the not-so-distant future in order to haggle over twenty years of accumulated stuff, but for now, a note on the back of an envelope was all I was willing to give him.

I bit my lip and shifted my weight from one foot to the other, dreading the final goodbyes. "I should probably load up the van and get on the road."

Laurel glanced at CiCi, and they exchanged a look.

Laurel ran her tongue over her teeth, biting back a smile. "Funny you should mention that."

CiCi's eyes sparkled with laughter. "Yeah, hilarious. So, I was telling Marcus about the whole deal last night."

I arched a brow. Marcus, her husband, was one of my closest and oldest friends. He also owned the local Porsche dealership.

"And?" I was a little embarrassed that she'd told him about it, but we'd all known each other since college. Even though he was one of the guys, I had faith that he was absolutely on my side.

CiCi scowled. "And he was more than a little shocked that Ms. Bubbles was driving the Porsche. Rob just bought that yesterday, and Marcus assumed it was for you. Imagine his surprise when I explained where it actually went."

Rage bubbled up in me, red and hot. I should've realized that since I was the one who signed her paycheck every month. Though we paid her generously, it was nowhere near enough for her to afford any Porsche, let alone a brand-new one.

I ground my teeth. "You gotta be kidding me. I've been driving an eight-year-old minivan, and he buys her a Porsche?"

CiCi nodded. "To say Marcus was displeased is the understatement of the century. He feels like Rob used him because he asked for the friend rate, and Marcus gave it to him. So, since he still had your all's financials—and I do mean your all's, not just Rob's—he sent me over with a little parting gift."

She took me by the hand and led me over to the picture window.

I blinked several times, not quite sure I believed what I was seeing. A shiny slate-gray Mustang GT gleamed in the sun.

Laurel draped her arm around my shoulders, and CiCi grinned. "I have the paperwork for it in my briefcase. All you have to do is sign and write the check."

I'd always been a huge fan of Mustangs. I'd had an older-model one in college. Even though it had been a beater that burned oil faster than I could pour it in, it had been my pride and joy.

I put my hand to my throat and fiddled with my horseshoe necklace. "I don't know. I don't know what to say. I know we have quite a bit of money in savings, but I don't know if we have enough for that."

Laurel rolled her eyes. "You have more than enough in there. And technically, no divorce papers have been filed, so it's as much yours as it is his. And need I remind you he bought his little tart a brand-new Porsche?"

That was all it took. "Where do I sign?"

Smiling, she reached for her briefcase, popped it open, and pulled out a stack of papers. "Marcus already did all the paperwork, including the tag transfer. All you have to do is sign in a few spots, write a check, then switch tags."

She put the papers in front of me and pointed to the first signature line. When I saw the actual cost of the vehicle, my eyes about popped out of my head. "Is that really the price?"

CiCi nodded. "Yep. And before you start doing the math in your head, he paid more than twice that for her Porsche. Marcus would've sent one of those—and still will if that's what you like—but he knows how much you love Mustangs. He worked out a deal with a friend of his at the Ford dealership."

I made my way through the stack of paperwork, and five minutes later, I was the owner of a brand-new Mustang. I shoved aside a little niggle of guilt. The girls were right—I'd worked every bit as hard for that money as he had, and if he could dig into our savings for a Porsche for his girlfriend, he could come off the cash for a Mustang for his wife.

Once the deed was done, both girls scooped me into a hug, then pushed me back, their expressions bittersweet.

Laurel cleared her throat. "I guess all that's left to do is put your things in the car."

"I guess so."

I went upstairs and scooped all my cosmetics into a small box, then took a final look around at the house I'd raised my family in while the girls carried my suitcases down.

I felt a little guilty for leaving all the broken glass and signs of my temper tantrum, but the vision of Rob and Bubbles sitting on my couch pushed it away. To hell with it. They'd made the figurative mess, so they could clean up the literal result. I had a brand-new life ahead of me.

Chapter Three

The drive from Atlanta to Dolphin Key took just over eight hours. I drove it straight through, only stopping when I had to pee. Laurel and CiCi had thought ahead and packed me snacks and even a couple of sandwiches to eat along the way, so I didn't have to waste time with that. Thank goodness for durable black leather seats.

When I was close, the GPS finally led me off of the highway and onto a road that meandered along the shoreline. Seagulls drifted lazily on the currents over the ocean, occasionally diving down to pluck dinner from the water. I knew I was getting close when beachside shops started popping up, at first sporadically, then so thick I could no longer see the ocean despite being only a couple of football fields away.

A cheerful white wooden sign with a pair of jumping dolphins flanked by palm trees welcomed me to town, and my stomach fluttered a little bit when I saw it. This was it. I just crossed the border into my new hometown. I had to admit, the wide expanse of blue skies dotted with a few puffy white clouds and the little stores painted in various pastel colors had a much more happy-go-lucky feeling than the skyscrapers of Atlanta. Rather than sidewalks full of hustling people avoiding eye contact, families and couples strolled past storefronts, taking their time and enjoying the experience. My heart smiled, and for the first time since Rob had set me down and shattered life as I knew it, I felt hopeful.

A mile or so past the welcome sign, my GPS—which I'd switched to a sexier-than-Rob man's voice—informed me that my destination was on the right. I flipped on my blinker and turned into a gravel parking lot large enough to hold twenty cars, max. I pulled up into the empty spot directly in front of the doors and took a second to look around. A wind-worn wooden porch spanned the entire front of the building, offering shade and rocking chairs to incoming guests. Round pine posts supported it, and the faded blue wooden siding looked welcoming rather than rundown. True to the overall look of the town, the window frames were painted a cheerful pink, and a yellow doorframe drew the eye immediately to the front entrance.

It could do with some sprucing up, maybe some flowers and a fresh coat of paint, but overall, I liked the relaxed vibe. Birds of Paradise trees flanked either side, and palm trees swayed toward the back. The not-so-distant ocean whispered in the background amidst strains of "Cheeseburger in Paradise." Something about the whole thing soothed my soul, as if the ocean air was absorbing my hurt and replacing it with peace.

Since my new home was an apartment above the bar, I was glad to see that the building was decent sized. I didn't need much space, but I didn't want to be squeezed into a shoebox either. I stepped out of the car, and a little thrill shot through me when I reached down and touched the door handle to lock my shiny new car. My girls had sent me off in style in a car that symbolized my future rather than reminded me of my past.

As I made my way inside the bar, I was surprised to see that the entire back of the building had garage doors that rolled up and down so that the building could be wide open to the back or closed to suit the weather. Wood-plank floors rubbed smooth by years of sandy feet were mirrored by tongue-and-groove walls and open-beam ceilings.

Overall, even though it was dark, the room had a feeling of spaciousness and heart. A few pool tables, air hockey tables, and foosball tables sat on either side of the main walkway that led to the back, and a small bar area sat in the corner. From the looks of it, though, it didn't get used very often. If I had to venture a guess, the only time it saw much action was when the weather was too bad to be outside. I smiled when I realized that probably wasn't that often.

Jimmy Buffett's "Cheeseburger in Paradise" floated in on the ocean breeze blowing through the open back doors, and laughter rang out. A ramp sloped from the main indoor walkway down onto a wooden deck. I strolled past a shuffleboard area and smiled when I saw two couples playing cornhole off to my left.

A huge, round tiki bar squatted behind them right at the edge of the sand with nothing but a long stretch of beach that led to the ocean as its background.

I climbed onto an empty bar stool and smiled at the handful of other guests, glad I'd made a last-minute wardrobe change from navy slacks and a button-down shirt to khaki shorts and the cheery green tank top the girls had bought me. As a final show of defiance, I'd crammed the stuffy clothes into the rest-area garbage bin as I'd headed back to my car.

A tall, well-built man with longish red-blond hair and a couple days' stubble stood over a double sink washing bar glasses, muscles flexing with his movement as he chatted with the man and woman in front of him. With his build and the way he had his hair pulled into a short ponytail at the nape of his neck, he reminded me of one of the Scottish warriors on the front of my memaw's bodice rippers.

He turned his head and glanced at me over his shoulder, then flashed me a smile that held just a hint of danger and promise. Yummy. My dormant libido stirred to life before I could remind myself that this man was my employee. He carried himself with an easy confidence that bordered on arrogance, and I found myself intrigued. I resisted the silly urge to fan myself.

He slid a coaster and a laminated menu in front of me. "Hey, there. Welcome to the Tipsy Flamingo. What can I get you?"

My mouth went a little dry as he pinned me with blue eyes so dark that they reminded me of the sea whooshing in the background. I did a mental head-shake and returned his smile. Clearing my throat, I started to order a white wine before I remembered where I was at. "I'll have a top-shelf margarita on the rocks, salted rim, please."

He winked and smiled. "Comin' right up."

His voice held a tinge of an accent, but he hadn't said enough for me to decide what it was. I studied him while he made my drink and tried to get ahold of myself. I wasn't one of those lecherous cougars who ogled men for fun, and I sure wasn't some giggling school girl, but this guy was sex on a stick, and the worst part was that I didn't even get the feeling he was trying. I finally wrote it off to the emotional upheaval of the last several days piled on top of my fresh-found giddiness at starting a new life in this amazing place.

I debated asking to speak to a manager right off the bat but decided to sit and observe for a while before I made my identity known. I figured it wouldn't hurt to do some quiet observation while I got a handle on the place. See what went down when the boss wasn't around, so to speak, and I wasn't ready to dive straight into business yet, anyway. Afternoon was fading to evening, and I wasn't even sure I was ready to spend the night in a place haunted by my dad's presence. A hotel sounded better all the time, and since I'd stopped at the bank and transferred another fifty grand into my own brand-new checking account—the difference between my Mustang and her Porsche because fair is fair—I could afford it.

I sat back and tried to be objective as an employer rather than a woman admiring a ridiculously hot guy as he made my margarita. I'd bartended my way through college, so even though that had been two decades ago, it was as fresh in my mind as if it were yesterday. Regular margarita nights with the girls and frequent cocktail parties to schmooze clients had kept my mixing skills sharp. I mentally counted as he poured the booze, pleased when he used the correct measures. Nothing cut into profits faster than heavy-handed bartenders.

He slid the drink in front of me, those blue eyes sending a tingle through me. "One top-shelf margarita. I'm Ronan. Are you hungry? Our wings are the best around, and the po' boy is made with locally sourced shrimp."

Since I was an utter slob when it came to wings, I decided to go with the sandwich. The last thing I wanted was to drop buffalo sauce or blue cheese down my front. Not the best first impression, and compared to the easy grace with which he moved, I felt a little like a pregnant llama.

He tilted his head when I ordered. "Where're you from? I'd say Savannah if I had to guess."

I smiled as I squeezed the orange wedge into my drink. "Close. Atlanta. Now, your turn. Where are you from?"

One side of his mouth curved into a small smile. "Scotland originally, but I've been here long enough that I've lost the accent. I've been in this area for a while now."

"Hey, Ronan! Stop flirtin' and introduce us!" Two middle-aged men in brightly colored Aloha shirts grinned at me from their stools catty-corner to me. "She doesn't look like a tourist, but she's not from around here either."

Normally, nosiness bugged me, but this man radiated genuineness and an honest curiosity. "I'm Jules. I just moved here from Atlanta."

He beamed at me. "I'm Eddie, and this is my husband Erik." He motioned to an adorable Puggle lying fast asleep on the cool bricks between their stools. "And this is Cerbi. We moved here from Ohio five years ago and haven't looked back. You say you just moved here. How long ago? We haven't seen you around, and we'd have noticed."

Ronan barked out a laugh as he leaned a lean hip casually against the center island and crossed his arms. "And that's the truth. When he says they moved here from Ohio, he means *here* literally. They pretty much live on those two stools."

I smiled and moved to a stool closer to the couple. I could tell already that they were chatty, so there was no need to continue hollering across the bar. I tried to keep a straight face as I took a sip of my drink. "I've lived here for almost twenty minutes."

Erik's brown eyes turned up at the corners in good

humor. "That long, huh? You're almost a local. What brings you here?"

I raised a brow. "What makes you think I had a reason? Maybe I just decided I wanted to live somewhere warmer."

Eddie flapped a hand. "Sugar, people enjoy the weather once they get here, but there's almost always a story that precipitates the move. What's yours?"

Erik frowned at him and swatted him on the arm. "Stop bein' nosy. You just met the poor thing, and you're already tryin' to drag her business out."

I sighed, surprised to find myself wanting to tell the story. I was normally a private person, but here I was, in a strange place not knowing a soul. I had a feeling these two were going to become an important part of my life if they were here as often as Ronan claimed.

I took another long pull from my drink. "No, it's okay. The long and short of it is that my husband of twenty years traded me in for a younger model, and I didn't wanna stick around and be the jilted woman everybody stared at and whispered about. For a big city, Atlanta's a very small town, and I figured a fresh start was the way to go."

Cerbi, bless his heart, got up and came to me, then put his head against my leg as if to comfort me. Dogs were so awesome. Eddie and Erik exchanged a knowing look, and I was glad to see there wasn't an ounce of pity in their gazes when they turned back to me. If anything, I picked up a sense of outrage for me.

Eddie flapped a hand. "Well, honey, his loss. I'm an excellent judge of character, and I can already tell you're gonna be one of the family. Right, Ronan?"

I glanced at the man leaning behind the bar. Though he was still, a sort of coiled energy radiated from him. I'd never felt that in another person, and it was a little unsettling. His gaze was so intense as he studied me that I had to resist the urge to squirm and look away.

Finally, he spoke. "It's definitely his loss. No man in his right mind leaves a woman for a girl, and we're glad to have you. I hope you find what you're looking for here."

His tone was soft and carried almost the same weight as a physical caress. That sounds weird, but it's the closest I can come to describing it. A cloak of serenity I hadn't experienced since before I'd left to take Bryan to college surrounded me, and the lump of rage and hurt I'd been carrying in my gut fizzled to an ember. I drew my first stress-free breath in a week, and though I hadn't expected such a rapid change, I welcomed it.

I pulled in a deep breath, suddenly feeling guilty for keeping my identity a secret from people who were being kind to me. That was no way to start new relationships, and I sighed. It was time to bring that to the light of day.

Chapter Four

I finished my drink in one final gulp, figuring if worse came to worst, I could Uber to a hotel. "I have to confess something, guys. I'm not starting my life here with secrets or dishonesty. I've had enough of that to last me a lifetime."

Ronan slid my po' boy in front of me. "Whatever it is can't be that bad. No offense, but you don't strike me as a person who could do anything too horrible."

Eddie grinned. "You don't know that. Maybe she killed her husband before she left. Or maybe he's tied up in their backyard with his dangly bits covered in honey."

Ronan furrowed his brow and blinked hard a couple times. "What the hell's wrong with you, Ed? I'm sure he's alive and well, man parts and all." He turned to me, slightly less confident. "Right?"

Erik rolled his eyes. "Of course he is. Our girl's no murderer no matter how much somebody has it comin'. I can just tell."

I smiled. "Though the thought did briefly cross my

mind, no, I didn't kill my husband. I did kill his big-screen TV, though."

"Then he should count himself lucky," Eddie replied, taking a swig of his draft beer. "I can't abide a cheater."

Without asking, Ronan made another margarita and set it in front of me, smiling. Thankfully, he didn't have the cliche dimples—that would have just been over the top.

I reached out to pull the glass toward me, and our fingers brushed. Instinctively, I yanked my hand back as a little charge of electricity similar to static shock zipped up my fingers. He jumped, then shoved his hands in his pockets, suspicion and curiosity flickering across his features before he could school his expression back to neutral.

"Maybe you should tell us the rest of the story now." He never took his eyes off me, and something in the dark blue depths made me feel exposed, like he was reading my soul.

I shook that off as nerves. "My whole name is Jules Cavanaugh. I'm Arnie Cavanaugh's daughter." I'd made the decision to take back my maiden name on the way down here. I had no desire to tarnish my do-over by thinking of Rob every time I signed my name.

Ronan's gaze whipped toward mine again, and his jaw worked a couple times before words came out. "Wait, what? Daughter? But Arnie didn't have any kids. Are you sure ... Peterson said the bar was being sold."

I curved my lips into a self-deprecating smile as I traced the condensation ring on the bar with my finger. "Though I shouldn't be surprised he never mentioned me, Arnie did indeed have a daughter. I'm sure." I spread my arms wide. "Ta-da! And yeah, I'd planned to sell it, but that was before my husband upended my life."

Ronan's face went red, and he scrubbed a hand over his face before turning on his heel and stomping into the back.

Eddie leaned forward on his elbow, dropping his chin into his hand. "Oh, my. This has taken a turn for the dramatic. Girl, your stock just went up twenty points in my book just for bein' able to strike Ronan speechless. Way to bury the lede."

Erik arched a brow and rubbed the back of his sunburned neck. "Wowzer, though. You sure put a bee in his bonnet. I don't think I've ever seen him rattled."

I plucked a shrimp from atop my sandwich and popped it into my mouth, then dragged a fry through the puddle of ketchup I'd squirted onto the red-and-white checkered paper. The relief that had spread through me a few minutes before remained. "I think we just surprised him. He strikes me as a person who's used to being in control of every situation, so this is probably a lot."

Eddie cringed. "I'm glad you see that, sweetie, because you're gonna need a heapin' helpin' of empathy. He'd just told us yesterday that he'd decided to buy the place."

I closed my eyes and swore. This wasn't the way I'd seen my first day going, but I don't suppose I should have been surprised. Somebody—Ronan apparently—had been running it for a month with no oversight, and now that I knew I'd crushed his dreams, well, I felt like a jerk.

I worked up a solid apology in my mind as I chatted with Eddie and Erik and worked my way through my sandwich. I was going to need Ronan, so we had to find a way forward. I'd just popped the last french fry in my mouth when two young women in bikinis made their way directly from the beach to the bar. The first, a blonde with freckles spattered across her sunburned cheeks, leaned on the bar and stood on her tiptoes, peering toward the back.

"Where's Ronan?" she asked without taking her eyes off the dark space that she was obviously expecting to spit out the hottie bartender. I grinned at her naivety as Eddie winked at me. Ronan was so far out of her league that they weren't even in the same sport. I knew without question she'd never make it through the first encounter.

The other girl, a brunette that reminded me a little too much of Bubbles, adjusted her almost-too-small, blue polka-dotted top and huffed out a breath. "We don't have all day. Our stuff's still down on the beach."

"I'm sure he'll be right back," I said, suppressing a grin.

When the girls had waited a solid three minutes and Ronan still hadn't emerged from the back, they started to get impatient.

The blonde shifted her weight from one foot to the other, and I could sense her impatience growing. I couldn't blame her. Three minutes was a long time to wait for a drink when you had the beach calling.

When he didn't reappear after another minute, I shot a questioning look at Erik and Eddie, who both shrugged.

I bit my lip. I didn't want to overstep, especially considering I'd already pushed Ronan's buttons, but I also didn't want to lose the sale.

I pushed off my stool and headed around the bar. "I'm sure he'll be right back, but what can I get you?"

Disappointment etched her face, but her need for another drink outweighed her desire to have it served by two hundred pounds of hotness. Thankfully, they were only drinking frozen margaritas, so I didn't have to pull any recipes from the deep, dark dungeon of my long-term memory. My problem, however, was that I had no idea how much to charge.

Erik came to my rescue. "You ladies came for refills just in time. Happy hour ends in fifteen minutes, and then margaritas go from five dollars to eight."

I shot him a grateful look as I pushed the drinks across the counter to the girls. "That'll be ten dollars."

My next issue was that I had no idea how to work the register. It required a numeric passcode just to access the system, so I couldn't have worked it even if I'd understood how to ring up the drinks anyway. Instead, I slid the money under the edge of the register, then went back to my seat.

"Is he usually gone this long?"

Eric pressed his lips together and shook his head. "Never. He seems to have some sort of sixth sense when it comes to new customers. His service is always top notch."

We chatted about the area for a few minutes, but the longer Ronan was gone, the more antsy I got. Images of him lying in the back unconscious from a fall got the better of me. "I want to go check on him."

Eddie nodded. "I think that's a good idea."

I made my way back behind the bar and stepped tentatively into the back area. "Ronan?"

When I didn't get a response, I called for him again even though the area was open and I would've surely seen him had he been there. I wound my way around boxes and shelves of liquor and caught sight of a large silver door that I assumed was a walk-in refrigerator. Maybe he was locked inside, though my memory of them was that the door opened from inside as well as out.

Pulling the handle to unlatch the door, I was almost afraid of what I'd find in there. I needn't have worried, though. There was nothing inside except what you would expect: produce, dairy, and plastic bins of prepped food.

Making sure the door closed behind me, I looked around. There was one other door that I assumed led to an office. I knocked, and when I didn't get a response, I shoved the door open. The neat freak in me about had a stroke.

Files and loose sheets of paper were scattered across the desk, and bank boxes were stacked all over the place. A safe squatted in one corner, and a whiteboard with names and dates that I assumed was the schedule hung on one wall. I left the room, careful to close the door behind me.

The only other option was a door with a lighted exit sign over the top. I sighed, beginning to suspect that I'd been ditched. I squinted in the bright sunlight when I opened the door. All that was out there was a fenced area and a big green dumpster.

Irritated beyond measure, I made my way back to the bar. Eddie and Erik peered at me expectantly, their glasses empty.

I shrugged. "He's gone. It looks like I'm on my own. Let me get you two another beer, and then I'll figure out what to do."

Eddie motioned toward a silver cooler with sliding doors on top beside the sink. "The frozen mugs are in there."

Eric rubbed the back of his neck, scowling. "Ronan's an awesome guy, but it's pretty shitty of him to just leave you stuck here. If it helps, Austin should be here in an hour or so. He's your evening relief and has been here forever. He'll be able to walk you through shift change."

I pulled in a deep breath and blew it out, pushing down my irritation and mild panic as I went back around and resumed my seat. "Thank heaven for small blessings."

We had a few customers over the next half an hour, but they kept it simple. Since I had no idea how to work anything in the kitchen or even what was on the menu, I had to turn one couple away. Killing somebody with food poisoning on my first day didn't feel like sound business practice to me.

Erik caught my attention as I was stacking glasses in the

freezer and motioned toward the main building. "Looks like you're in luck."

"He's early. That's Austin," Eddie said as a tall, thin guy that I put in his mid-thirties strode toward us, tying a black apron over his blue-plaid board shorts. Full-sleeve tattoos covered both arms and crept beneath the sleeves of a dark blue T-shirt with the bar's logo on the back.

A grin spread across his face as he pulled his dark hair up into a man bun. "Hey, guys," he said to Erik and Eddie. He nodded at me, his expression friendly but curious. "Not that I mind coming in to find an attractive, smiling woman behind the bar, but where's Ronan?"

I arched a brow. "That seems to be the question of the hour."

His brow furrowed in confusion. "I don't follow."

Eric pulled in a deep breath and blew it out through pursed lips. "You're not the only one. Maybe we should bring you up to speed."

I stuck out my hand. "I'm Jules. The long and short of it is that I'm Arnie's daughter, and I just moved here from Atlanta. When I told Ronan that, he stormed out, and we haven't seen him since. That was about forty-five minutes ago, and he's nowhere to be found."

Austin stroked his little goatee. "I can see where he would've been upset, but I'm surprised he just left. His truck's not out front, though, so he obviously did." He shrugged and smiled at me. "Fortunately, making margaritas when life gives you limes is one of my strong suits. If you want a crash course, I'm more than happy to give you one. And by the way, welcome to Dolphin Key and the Tipsy Flamingo."

I wasn't happy about it, but the situation could have been much worse. "Trial by fire. I guess I'm in."

I joined him behind the bar and spent the next few hours learning the ropes so I could work my first official shift the next day if Ronan had decided to call it quits permanently. It looked like my new life was off to a running start.

Chapter Five

By the time midnight rolled around, I was dead on my feet. The shrimp po' boy, the only real food I'd eaten all day, had long since worn off, and my tank was empty.

Even though it was a Tuesday, we'd had a steady flow of customers—just enough that I was able to learn the register and the basics about the menu without being overwhelmed. Thankfully, everything was either deep-fried or made from lunchmeat, so even if I had to run the place by myself, there wasn't much of a learning curve.

After the last guest left, Austin laid his hand on my shoulder. "You look like you're ready to pass out. We don't usually close until two, but it's slow enough tonight that I think we can get away with shutting it down now. Are you up to learning the closing side duties, or would you rather put that off 'til tomorrow?"

I thought for a second. I was exhausted, but if Ronan didn't show up the next day, I had to open the place. "I'm beat, so it would be awesome to put it off. Between not getting much sleep last night, driving eight hours to get here, and being on my feet for the last five hours, I don't have much left. But considering the circumstances, you better show me now. And if you could give me the bare-bones on opening in the morning, that would be fantastic."

He squeezed my shoulder. "I have a better idea. Why don't we work on closing duties tonight, and I can come in to help you open tomorrow. Honestly, though, I think Ronan will show up. He probably just needed a little bit of breathing space and time to process. Despite what he did today, he's a good guy and is dedicated to the bar."

I gave him a grateful smile. "Are you scheduled to work tomorrow night? I don't want to make you pull a double."

He shook his head. "Nope. Tomorrow is my day off, but I don't mind coming in and at least getting you started."

It was nice to know I had at least one employee I could depend on.

Austin frowned at me as he moved the clean glasses to the freezer. "You didn't tell me you just got here today. Had I known that, I would've cut you some slack."

I shook my head as I wiped off the bar. "It's no big deal. Being busy was probably the best thing for me."

He peered at me over his shoulder as he situated the mugs. "Feel free to tell me if it's none of my business, but what brought you here? We didn't even know you existed, let alone that you were coming down to take over the business."

I gave him a wry smile as I tossed the bar towel into a bucket of sanitizer and leaned against the cooler. "I didn't even realize I was coming down to take over the business. To be honest, my plan was to sell the place without even coming down to look at it. To say Arnie and I didn't have the best relationship would be the understatement of the year. He left when I was ten, and I haven't laid eyes on him since

I was thirteen. My situation ... changed suddenly, though, and Florida suddenly seemed like the place I needed to be."

He nodded as he pulled the plugs from sinks so they could drain. "You'd be amazed by how many people end up here with that same exact story. The details might be different, but this seems to be a place where people come to start over."

I was grateful when he didn't ask for any more details. Between exhaustion and the stress of Ronan walking out, I'd have turned into a sobbing puddle of goo if I'd had to rehash the events of the last few days.

Once we had the bar clean and stocked, he showed me how to pull down the security doors around the tiki and chain the chairs together so nobody would steal them.

"These stools weigh a ton. People really steal them?" I rubbed my aching back as I pushed the padlock closed and stood.

He nodded. "Yep, believe it or not, they do. We came in here one morning, and four of them were missing. We found them later down the beach, but hauling them back was a pain. It's easier just to chain them and call it a day."

I sighed and limped my way back around the bar and followed him to the back.

He pushed the office door closed and locked it behind us just as he had the door leading from the bar. "Where are you staying tonight? I mean, you own the apartment right here, so all you have to do is take that flight of stairs and crash."

I sagged into the chair behind the desk even though I was moderately worried I wouldn't be able to get back out of it. On top of the exhaustion, my knees and feet were killing me. As bad as I hated to admit it, forty-nine-year-old me didn't have the same get up and go twenty-year-old me had enjoyed. In fact, it had gotten up and went about four hours ago. "My plan had been to get a hotel room and deal with the apartment tomorrow, but the idea of even walking to my car makes me want to cry."

He gave me a sympathetic smile as he pulled a chair around and took a seat beside me. "The apartment's been closed up for a month, but Arnie was a bit of a neat freak. I have no doubt it's in fine shape if you want to stay there."

It wasn't my first choice, but it was free and close. It occurred to me that I hadn't received any keys since I hadn't expressed an interest in coming down. I said as much.

Austin plucked a key ring holding seven keys off the desk. "No worries there. Ronan might've walked out like an ass, but at least he left you the keys. You have the apartment key, the ones for the front and back doors of the main building, the keys to unlock the shutters and chairs around the tiki, and the keys for this building and the office." He pointed to each one. "See? They're all labeled for you."

"Another small blessing. At least this day wasn't a total shit show. That does beg the question of whether or not he's planning to show up tomorrow, though. I mean, why leave keys?" I shook my head. "That's a problem for tomorrow-me, though. Right-now me just wants to crash on the nearest soft surface."

I wasn't keen on sleeping in a bed that most likely had dirty sheets, but I was confident there was a couch, and right then, that was all I needed.

Ten minutes later, we finished up the paperwork, and he cast me a concerned look. "Are you okay going upstairs by yourself, or do you want me to go show you around?"

My lips curled up into a tired half smile. "I'm pretty sure I can find the sofa, and that's about all the energy I have left to do. Thanks a ton for all your help and for being willing to come in and help me open tomorrow."

He waved me off. "It was no problem at all. You caught on quick, so I have no doubt you'll be up and running in no time. Let me at least help you carry your stuff up if you haven't already."

That was an offer I wasn't going to refuse. Since I hadn't brought much, it only took a few minutes. Once inside the apartment, he drew his brows down and scraped his fingers across his five-o'clock shadow. "Wow. I had no idea Arnie remodeled this place, but this is nothing like what it looked like the last time I was up here."

I lifted a tired shoulder. "Honestly, right now, I'd be happy if it had nothing in it but a couch. Thanks again for your help, and I'll see you tomorrow."

After seeing him out and locking the door behind him, I sagged against the door and got my first glimpse of my new home. My eyes rounded as I took in the place. Unlike my house, which I'd meticulously decorated with modern, upscale furniture and fancy art befitting a high-level executive's home, my father had obviously shared my love of a more relaxed decor.

The living room, dining area, and kitchen was open-concept. An overstuffed, cream-colored sofa and two matching recliners squatted in the living room around a glass-topped wicker coffee table, and a modern but warm cinnamon-colored marble bar flecked with gold and black separated the kitchen from the living room. Tall maple cabinets above and below curved around the stainless-steel double sink and flat-top stove and ended at a new brushed stainless-steel refrigerator.

Touches of beach decor—a basket of seashells here and a few beach scene paintings there—complemented the light-gray walls and made the place feel even homier. All in all, the place was cheery and much better on the eyes than I'd expected. In fact, it was exactly how I'd have decorated it in my imagination.

I tottered toward the couch and collapsed onto it, and by the time my head hit the overstuffed blue throw pillow, I was out like a light.

Thanks to a bladder that had shrunk three sizes over the years, I woke up at four a.m. and stumbled through the house until I found the bathroom. I didn't notice until too late that the toilet paper holder held nothing but an empty cardboard roll. I sighed and rubbed my forehead, seriously contemplating drip drying. That was gross, though, so I contorted around the sink and pulled open the cabinet, hoping to catch a break and find a few rolls in there. For once, luck was with me.

After I washed my hands and made my way back to the living room, my brain was awake and processing the details of the day before. I laid back down on the couch, but after tossing and turning for fifteen minutes, I gave up the ghost and pushed to a sitting position. I'd learned a long time ago that once my mind was awake, my body couldn't override it.

I wandered around the house, familiarizing myself with it. I was surprised to find two bedrooms rather than one, and even more shocked that the warm, beachy, almost feminine feel of the place extended to them. Maybe my dad had hired a designer or gotten a hand from a female friend.

I stepped into the master bedroom, feeling a little bit like a voyeur in the private space. I trailed my fingers over the reclaimed-wood furniture and then took a seat on the king-size bed, enjoying the feel of the gray Sherpa blanket. I'd always wanted one of those, but it hadn't fit my decor.

I took a minute to look around, absorbing the soothing

ambience until I noticed a painting of a long dock stretching out into the ocean. The print was slightly crooked, which bugged the crap out of me to the point that I had to get up and straighten it. Much to my surprise, the whole thing swung outward when I touched it, revealing a safe with a combination lock.

On a whim and a gut feeling, I spun the lock using my birthdate and was flabbergasted when it worked. Tilting my head, I pulled the heavy door open and examined the contents. Much like my own safe, it held a couple manila envelopes, a cash box, and a jewelry box, though where mine was cedar, this one was smooth acacia. The first two items didn't surprise me much, but the jewelry box did, for some reason.

I glanced over my shoulder instinctively, as if my father's ghost would appear and bust me snooping, before I reached in and pulled the box out. If I hadn't known better, I would've sworn it warmed under my fingers. Thumbing the little latch sideways, I lifted the lid and gasped when I saw one of the most beautiful necklaces I'd ever laid eyes on. I recognized it as the Tree of Life set in a filigreed silver circle, and the roots were wrapped around an oblong ruby. Rather than being on a chain, it was on a strip of black velvet and had a silver clasp. Like the box, the stone seemed to warm in my hand. I admired it for a minute, then put it back and set it aside.

Hoping the manila envelopes held documents that would give me more information about the bar and property, I reached for them. When I realized they were sitting atop a picture album and a thick, leather-bound book, my curiosity got the better of me, and I pulled the book out. The mystery tome was preferable to a photo album since I wasn't quite ready to take a trip down memory lane. Even after years of on-again-off-again therapy, it pained me to admit I was an almost-fifty-year-old woman with daddy and abandonment issues. Since the recent events in my life had already turned me into an emotional eggshell, that particular can of worms could stay closed.

The book was another story though. It had no title, but each outer corner was protected by delicate filigreed gold caps. What appeared to be hand-painted gold rune symbols decorated the front, surrounding an image that mirrored the necklace, complete with what I assumed was a real ruby inset into the leather. I ran my fingers over it and blinked when some trick of the light made the stone appear to glow at my touch. Writing that off as a trick of an exhausted mind, I flipped through the pages, surprised to find them aged but blank. When I closed the cover, the ruby winked at me again.

I closed my eyes and took a couple deep breaths. Obviously, my brain was overloaded to the point that I was hallucinating. I smiled as an image of the Book of Shadows from the TV series *Charmed* flashed through my mind. I loved supernatural shows and read urban fantasy books like they were my religion. If only magic were real, and a book could bless me with gifts that would sweep me away from the shit show that was currently my life. It was probably better it wasn't, though. I wasn't sure I could contain myself if I really had the ability to shrink Rob's junk, zip his lying lips shut, or explode his tiny head. With great power comes great responsibility, and I wasn't feeling particularly responsible.

I shook my head to clear the fluff but allowed myself one final fantasy—me, twenty pounds lighter and smoking hot at my divorce hearing with Rob on his knees begging for forgiveness and Bubbles crying in the background, jealous. I pulled in a breath and blew it out, reminding myself that I was fine just the way I was, and that his cheating was no reflection on me. Easier said than believed, but if I repeated it enough, maybe that stupid, insecure voice in my head would shut up.

Shoving the book back into the safe, I pushed the door shut, swung the picture back into place, and left the bedroom, flipping the light off behind me. Though I hadn't even looked in the envelopes or cash box, it would keep.

I hobbled back down the hallway toward the kitchen, wincing when my body creaked and groaned with half a dozen aches and pains. I was too old and too out of shape to spend five hours rushing around a bar. Sleeping on the couch with my neck twisted up on an oversized pillow probably hadn't helped either.

I rolled my head, trying to work out some of the stiffness as I debated whether to make coffee or try to get a couple more hours' sleep. Experience told me coffee was probably the way to go because the odd contents of the safe were swirling around in my melon. Since the cabinets were probably empty, I was glad CiCi and Laurel had included a bag of my favorite beans in their goody bag.

I was shocked but grateful to find what appeared to be a brand-new espresso machine on the counter and a bottle of Advil in the cabinet. What I didn't have was milk, but I did have access to an entire restaurant worth of supplies. I slipped on my flip-flops and snuck down the dark stairwell to the walk-in fridge to filch a gallon. Maybe this whole living-above-a-bar thing would come in handy after all.

Chapter Six

I was tickled pink to discover the apartment had a balcony with a beach view complete with white wicker furniture similar to what I had in my breakfast nook at the old house. It brought back some great memories of doing homework with the boys and having margarita nights with the girls, and I found myself looking forward to showing all of them my new life. I'd texted Laurel and CiCi when I arrived the night before to let them know I'd gotten here, but I hadn't really given them many details. To make up for that, I spent some time snapping pictures and then sent them to them even though I knew they were both still in bed.

Since I was on the West Coast of Florida, there was no sunrise to see, but as night turned to dawn, I contemplated my new life as I watched seagulls diving for their breakfast and dolphins rolling not too far off the beach. Or at least I hoped they were dolphins. I didn't have much beach experience, so they could have been sharks. I shuddered. Death by Jaws was a recurring nightmare of mine.

I also knew I needed to tell the boys what was happening, but I wasn't quite sure how to go about it. They'd both just started their terms, and I didn't want to distract them with Rob's shitty life decisions or my hasty relocation. Bryan, especially, was sensitive to change, and this was his first year. His life was already turned upside down, and it killed me to know I was going to suck the joy out of what should be the greatest time of his life. I preferred for them to hear it from me, though, so I fired off a text asking for a FaceTime chat this afternoon.

I reflected over the events of the previous day. My first twelve hours here hadn't gone exactly to plan, but then again, I hadn't really had a plan. With the exception of Ronan, I was pleasantly surprised with the entire scenario. I'd been a little worried that the place would be rundown or, maybe worse yet, some sort of pulsing nightclub that attracted college kids on eternal spring break. Speaking of nightmares, that would've been one of epic proportions.

The apartment had been a pleasant surprise too. In fact, I couldn't have designed it better myself, right down to the spacious quad-head shower in the master bath. It was the bathing equivalent of surround-sound, and I'd always wanted that kind of setup. As soon as I discovered it, I couldn't resist, even though I hadn't finished my first cup of coffee. I felt gross from all the wear and tear from the day before, so the thought of hosing off all that grime—both physical and metaphorical—was too much to resist. The hot water soothed my aching muscles, and the citrus shampoo and body wash I found in the towel closet cleared my mind.

After messing around on social media for an hour as I sat on the deck and enjoyed my second latte, boredom set in, and my mind turned back to the contents of the safe.

Standing, I pulled the sliders open and slipped back inside, the smooth faux-wood tile cool under my bare feet as I padded back to the master bedroom.

Once I had the safe open, my gaze slid back and forth between the envelopes and the photo album. I bit my lip, drawn to the album but unwilling to take that deep dive into my childhood. I huffed out a breath and reached for it, feeling stupid because there probably weren't even any pictures of me in it.

I took it, the cash box, and the envelopes with me to the bed and climbed into the center of the plush blanket. Cross-legged, I opened the envelopes first.

The first one contained pretty much what I'd expected —a copy of the deed to the bar, the same will that his attorney had sent to me, and a copy of the life insurance policy I'd already collected on.

The second one was a little more confusing. There were several sheets of paper stapled together, but I couldn't read anything on them. They appeared to be in Latin, but since my fluency in that was basically nil beyond E Pluribus Unum and Semper Fi, I had no idea what they said. They weren't forms that looked familiar, either, so I shrugged and slid them back into the envelope.

I pulled in a deep breath and braced myself as I reached for the photo album. I needn't have bothered, though, because all the pictures had been snapped at the bar. Ronan, Eddie, Erik, and Austin appeared in many of them, smiling while wearing Halloween costumes, Santa hats, and sombreros that I assumed indicated they were celebrating Cinco de Mayo.

I smiled as I got a peek into moments of my father's life. After a couple pages, I noticed that in every single picture, he was wearing a signet-style ring that matched the tree-of-life necklace. The logical conclusion was that he'd had a matching pair made, but though there were numerous women who appeared in the photos, none of them wore it.

Though he was surrounded by friends, there didn't seem to be a constant woman present at all. That made me a little sad. Though he'd left me, I hadn't wished a life of loneliness on him. I tried to look deeper, studying his eyes and expressions for any sign of that, but he honestly appeared happy in all of them.

After I'd flipped past the last page, I closed it and pulled the money box toward me. I'd expected it to be locked, but apparently, he'd thought just keeping it in the safe was good enough. I slipped the little latch sideways and popped it open, then blinked a couple of times and about fell off the bed when I saw the contents. The first thing I slapped eyes on was two stacks of hundred-dollar bills.

I pulled the two banded groups of bills from the top of each stack, expecting to find smaller bills beneath it. Instead, it was more of the same. Five to each stack including the ones I pulled off the top, to be exact. I had enough caffeine rushing through my veins that my brain didn't have a problem doing the math on that one, especially since we were dealing with hundreds rather than fives. I'd just found a hundred grand in cold, hard cash.

Setting the money aside, I dug through the rest of the box to see if I might find some sort of explanation. Of course, all I found was another question. I used my fingernail to scoop a small silver key off the bottom of the box. Holding it up, I realized it was to a safety deposit box, but there was no name on it. I chewed on my lip while I thought about that.

Surely, it wouldn't be hard to track down the bank. It was most likely the same one that he did business with either personally or for the bar, so it appeared my next task would be figuring out what was more important than a hundred grand. After all, if he was comfortable keeping that much cash and a ruby big enough to choke a horse in the safe, whatever he put in the safety deposit box must be high value, indeed, though I had to wonder if it was sentimental rather than financial.

I dropped the key and the money back in the box, then carried everything back to the safe. I started to swing the door shut but paused, thinking. Ruby was my favorite stone, and I'd always wanted a tree-of-life necklace. The whole concept of Mother Earth and interconnectedness had always appealed to me, but Rob had always laughed at me and called it woowoo.

It felt a little invasive, but I reminded myself that this apartment and everything in it belonged to me now. Smiling, I reached for the jewelry box and wondered once again at the warmth of the wood as I lifted the lid open. The necklace lay just as I'd left it, and I admired it for a second before picking it up and clasping it around my neck.

When I turned to return the jewelry box to its proper place, my gaze caught on the thick old tome I'd flipped through and fantasized about the night before. Shoving the jewelry box back in the safe, I figured I'd examine the book a little closer. It was beautifully bound and in excellent condition, so it didn't make any sense to me that the pages were blank.

When my fingers brushed the leather cover, a weird sensation ran up my arm. It felt almost as if I was connecting with it. I shivered and pushed the feeling, as well as all the cool stuff running through my imagination, aside.

Rather than carry the book back to the bed, I slid it onto the edge of the reclaimed-wood dresser and flipped the front open. Unlike the night before, flowery script flowed across the center of the first page in a format that appeared to be a short poem. Or if we were living in one of my novels, a spell. Just for fun and to appease the fantasy fan inside me, I read the words aloud, complete with dramatic cadance.

* * *

Tempest rage
    Make me aware
    deep seas and lakes
    please hear my prayer

* * *

blessed fire
    healing earth
    come forth to me
    for my rebirth

* * *

As the last words left my lips, the fine hairs on my arms and nape of my neck stood up, and I would've sworn the parts of my body I could see pulsed with light for just a moment. I shuddered, then looked toward the window and laughed at my runaway imagination. Sunlight shone through the sheer curtains, bright and cheery. It must've bounced off the mirror in front of me and created an optical illusion.

I touched the necklace and admired how it looked. The stone set off my green eyes and looked good framed by my auburn hair, and the whole piece nestled perfectly in the hollow of my throat. For the first time in a week, despite the crow's feet and slight smudges under my eyes, I felt pretty.

Chapter Seven

I fiddled around with Facebook and Reddit, then completed my daily Pokemon Go task. It was a silly game, but Bryan had been a huge fan as a kid, and we'd started playing the game together. Now, it made me feel closer to him.

By the time another hour had passed, I was starting to feel a little claustrophobic. Since I'd likely work all day, I figured I'd better get out and go to the grocery store for some basics now. I was a little more excited than strictly necessary when a quick search revealed a Publix less than a block from me. It was my go-to grocery store in Atlanta, so at least one thing in my life wouldn't be changing.

After I finished my shopping, I spent a little time driving around town. It seemed like most of the businesses were clustered right along the shoreline, and the further inland you went, the more residential it became. Finding all the essential stores was a piece of cake, and it wasn't long before I began losing interest in exploring even though I was having a great time driving my new car.

I made a final stop at the drugstore for sunscreen. Even

though I hadn't had much sun exposure other than what I'd gotten the day before running drinks out to the patio tables, I was already a little sunburned. The last thing I needed was to blister and peel right off the bat in my new home.

The parking lot was still empty when I made it back to the bar, and I found myself glad I hadn't bought much. I'd have to keep in mind that I now lived in a place where I'd have to tote groceries for a hundred yards and then carry them up the steps. It would be wise to buy a little here and there rather than doing one massive weekly shop. The lazy side of me had no desire to make thirteen trips in humidity so thick it felt like I was breathing underwater.

With that in mind, rather than making two trips like I would have in the old house, I made a lazy man's load so I could get it all in one trip. It didn't take me long to put everything away, so I still had a couple of hours before I had to head down to the bar.

Lack of sleep was starting to catch up with me, and I considered grabbing a nap. I discarded the idea, though, because I knew myself well enough to know I'd just feel groggy and out of sorts when I woke up. Better to just muddle through, so I made myself a bagel and another cup of coffee and took my breakfast to the deck.

Temperatures had risen into the eighties, and the area that had been a nice respite that morning was now about the same temperature as the seventh circle of Hell. Thankfully, the table had a wide red umbrella, so I cranked it up and sank into a chair that faced the ocean. If this was how I'd get to spend my mornings, I was ready to go all in. I huffed a dry laugh through my nose, realizing that was a good thing considering I'd already flounced out of Atlanta. No way was I going back, tail tucked between my legs and begging Rob to let me stay in the house. Nope, I was a strong woman and the mistress of my own fate. I was gonna make this work or die trying.

A rush of feathers sweeping onto the deck railing startled me, and I jumped sideways, nearly falling out of my chair when one of the ugliest birds I'd ever seen swept onto the table, snatched my bagel, then hopped with it over to the railing.

My heart dropped back out of my throat once I realized nothing was gonna eat me, but annoyance coursed through me. I'd treated myself to the good honey cream cheese and had been looking forward to it. I glared as the dilapidated old parrot laid my bagel on the rail, lifted a wing, and scratched himself with his beak. He was missing some of his feathers, and I was pretty sure he was blind in one eye.

My anger dissipated a little as I realized the thing was so ancient that he was probably unable to catch his own food in the wild. "I'm willing to let that slide this time. You look like twenty miles of bad road, and I can relate to that today. I probably do too, or at least I feel like it."

That was the truth too. The Advil I'd taken earlier that morning was starting to wear off, and most every major muscle in my body was aching again. Bartending was hard work. Lifting, walking, twisting, bending—all the -ing words that my body just wasn't used to doing for long stretches.

The bird shifted his weight from one foot to the other and flapped his faded but still-colorful wings before settling into a relaxed, almost arrogant, hip-shot pose, ignoring the purloined bagel. He tilted his head, turning it slightly so that he was glaring at me with his good eye as he let out a loud squawk, then words. "Old hag!"

I arched a brow in surprise, and the little bit of the pity I'd felt for it slipped away. I'd dealt with enough pigeons at the park to know you either had to nip that in the bud or just accept that you were going to be harassed by a pushy bird with a sense of entitlement three times its size. I'd already been pushed as far in the last three days as I was willing to go, and I'd be damned if I was gonna take that level of shit from a bedraggled, mouthy old bird. A girl had to draw her line somewhere.

I pushed to my aching feet and took the few steps toward it, drawing myself up to my full height and narrowing my eyes. I jabbed a finger at him. "You look pretty comfortable there, so I'm gonna assume this is one of your regular roosts. We haven't met yet, but you have an obvious misconception of the peckin' order here."

I reached out and snatched the bagel back off the rail, but the bird was faster and more agile than I'd given it credit for. He snaked his neck out to take it back from me, but instead of grabbing the bagel, he got me on the thumb. Or maybe that's what he'd intended. I yelped, then smacked at it and yelled to shoo it away, determined not to get my ass kicked by a decrepit bird that was the squawking image of death warmed over.

When I refused to give up the food despite having lost a chunk out of my thumb, he came at me again. This time, I was ready for him, though. I tucked the bagel behind my back with one hand, then gave him my best roundhouse with the other. He was heavier than he looked, but I was shocked to see him fly clear over the railing. I stumbled sideways from the momentum as I shook my hand—it felt like I'd punched solid stone.

Before I could regain my balance, somebody cleared their throat behind me. Jumping, I spun around to face the new threat and dropped the bagel. The stupid bird must have been more durable than I'd thought too, because that punch should have knocked him for a loop. Instead, he swept back over the railing, snatched it off the deck, then flew to a tree a few yards away, casting what I would have sworn was a triumphant glance over his shoulder at me.

Ronan stood in the doorway to the house, his fist to his mouth. It didn't take a genius to figure out he was trying not to laugh.

My annoyance at the bird merged with my irritation at him for stomping out the previous day. I glared at him, struggling to maintain both my dignity and my hold on my temper. "I love that you found that amusing. What the hell are you doin' in my house? I didn't expect to see you again after you dipped on me yesterday."

He pressed his lips together and sighed. "I apologize for that. It was unprofessional and inconsiderate. My only excuse is that you caught me by surprise, to say the least. Also, I apologize for not being here to show you around and warn you that the bird bites. As far as what I'm doing here, I knocked, but you must not have heard me. When I heard you yelling through the door, I thought maybe somebody'd broken in. I know you have ... domestic issues going on right now, and I was worried about you."

That knocked me off my game a little. I'd expected belligerence or maybe arrogance, but not concern. In that light, I felt like I needed to be grateful to him, which was an irritation all its own. I wasn't over being mad at him for walking out and leaving me holding the bag.

"I'm perfectly able to take care of myself. While I appreciate the concern, my soon-to-be ex-husband is a cheatin' asshole, but he's not a wife beater. Besides, he has Bubbles to keep him company." I hated that I couldn't keep the bitterness from my voice.

"Beg pardon?" he asked, confusion etched on his angled features.

I sighed. "Bubbles. That's the name of our secretary and the woman he left me for. Her real name, actually, which somehow makes the kick to my pride a little harder."

I didn't want to taint this place with their images, so I glowered at the stupid parrot, who'd settled into the elbow of a nearby tree to enjoy my breakfast. "As far as the bird, I'll deal with him later. I have a feeling he's a regular fixture, so we're gonna have to establish some ground rules."

Ronan flat-out laughed. "Good luck with that. I've seen full-grown men take him on and come out on the bad end of it."

I gave him my sweetest smile. "I guess it's a good thing for me he's not dealing with just a full-grown man this time. Not so great for him, though."

Humor lit his blue eyes, lightening them to a shade that matched the Tipsy Flamingo T-shirt he was wearing. "I guess it's not, at that. Let me be the first to say that if anybody can take on Lapis and win, my money's on you."

I brushed off my clothes and reclaimed my seat under the umbrella. "I'd have had him if you hadn't interrupted me."

He held up his hands in surrender. "I have no doubt. That roundhouse was impressive. My apologies, both for this morning and for yesterday. How about we start over?"

I fluttered a careless hand and motioned toward the chairs at the table. "Honestly, my cup of drama currently runneth over. I came here for some peace and a fresh start, so in the spirit of that, pop a squat."

He took half a step back inside and reached for something. "Arnie didn't drink coffee, so I didn't figure he'd even have a coffee pot, let alone any beans. You struck me as a woman who loves her caffeine, so I figured I'd show up with a peace offering. I have a caramel latte and a plain black coffee because those are about the two safest ways to go. Take your pick unless you've had your fill."

Since I hadn't had a chance to touch the cup of coffee I'd brought outside with me, and it had gone cold during my struggle with the cantankerous old parrot, I smiled and took the latte. "Thank you."

We sat in silence for a few minutes, sipping our coffee and watching the ocean. I studiously ignored Lapis as he picked away at my bagel and decided instead to let it go. At least until next time.

"Where did you get that necklace?" Ronan asked, his intense gaze pinned to the jewelry at my throat.

My fingers fluttered to it. "I found it in my dad's stuff."

Considering there was a hundred grand stashed in the safe, it seemed prudent to keep my answer vague. I didn't know this man, and even though I knew he'd been here for years based on the photo album, I didn't know him from Adam.

He ran his tongue across his teeth, his expression a little guarded. "Just in his stuff? As in, casually tossed into a drawer? No note or anything?"

I swirled my cup, careful to keep my expression neutral even though the question was odd. "Something like that, and no, no note. Why?" Suddenly, it occurred to me that it might belong to somebody else as I'd originally suspected. Maybe she'd want it back. "Is there a particular reason you're curious about it?"

He started to say something, then swallowed. "No, no reason. It looks nice on you."

A few more minutes of silence crept by, but it had lost its easiness and had taken a turn toward uncomfortable. The scent of his cologne drifted toward me, and it was all I could do not to lean closer. It reminded me of the ocean breeze and clean laundry drying on a line. Tattoos that reminded me of the runes on the old book I'd found adorned his sculpted bicep and disappeared under his sleeve, and I licked my lips as I resisted the urge to follow them with my fingers. Places I hadn't even remembered I had started to get warm. What the hell was wrong with me?

Before I could get myself in trouble, I cleared my throat. "So Austin says my father must have remodeled this place. Whoever did it is amazing. I was a little worried it was going to be a true bachelor pad, but I couldn't be happier with the place if I'd designed it myself. He must have done it right before he died because the fridge and appliances seem brand new. The whole place does."

He tilted his head toward me. "How would Austin know?"

I laughed. Out of all I said, that was his takeaway. "He helped me bring my stuff up last night. By the way, thank you for leaving the keys, at least."

He blinked. "Not that I don't wish I would have, but I didn't leave the keys." He pulled a set from his pocket and dangled them from his finger.

I paused. "Then if you didn't leave them, who did?"

Before he could answer, Lapis made some sort of hacking sound that was halfway between a choke and hairball cough with such effort that he flapped his wings, sending even more feathers floating to the ground.

I smirked at him. "It serves you right, you old buzzard. Call me an old hag again."

I loved seeing Karma in action.

Chapter Eight

Despite the mess in the office, Ronan had kept meticulous books since Arnie had died. As he went over the ledgers with me, a little kernel of guilt settled in my gut. Less than twenty-four hours ago, he'd thought the place was going to be his. Now here he was, explaining the ropes to a woman he'd never met and who had no former attachment to the place. All things considered, he was being kinder and more generous than I would've expected from most people.

An hour into it, I rubbed my temples, fighting off a headache. He stopped what he was saying and gazed at me for a second. "I'm sorry. You have to be starving considering Lapis ate your breakfast. How inconsiderate of me. I guess this is a good time to show you around the kitchen."

I smiled, then winced when it hurt my head. "You're right—I am starving, but I got a pretty good trial by fire with the kitchen yesterday. Austin showed me the ropes."

When he drew his brows down, I realized I'd just taken an unintentional shot by reminding him that he left. I mentally shrugged, refusing to feel too guilty. He had, after all, bolted.

"Then I assume you know the menu fairly well," he said, his tone a little stiff.

I nodded once and decided to offer an olive branch. "I do, but you haven't eaten, either. Also, Austin didn't really show me the food rotations or fill me in on how much we keep prepped. If you could show me that, I'd appreciate it. I haven't worked in a bar in quite a few more years than my pride is willing to admit."

Ronan examined me for a minute, his eyes turning a smokier shade of blue-green that made me think of the sea after a storm. "I don't understand human women's obsession with youth. The only value in it is that it offers you the opportunity to make mistakes that shape you into a mature being who's worth getting to know. Have faith in yourself, Jules. Despite what your fool of a husband has made you believe, the years look good on you, inside and out."

The air around us seemed to crackle with the heat of his gaze, and I licked my suddenly dry lips. Intellect had always been a huge turn-on for me, and though my rational brain told me this stupidly hot man was just trying to be kind, my body—and the way his eyes fell to my lips—was telling me he meant every word.

My stomach growled, breaking the tension, and I smiled. "About that food..."

His shoulders relaxed. "I could eat. The rotation's pretty simple, really. Everything is labeled with a prep date and expiration date, so if you forget, you can just look at the time span on the last label or there's a chart in the walk-in. Most everything is two to five days."

We chatted about the area and my history as we made ourselves chicken patty sandwiches and onion rings. I smiled when I noticed he was eating two rather than one. I imagined it took quite a few groceries to feed a guy his size, and it was good to see a man with an appetite. Rob had gotten prissy with his eating over the years and would never consider eating anything out of a fryer, which meant I'd been missing out too, just from sheer convenience. Of course, since my metabolism had slowed down, that wasn't necessarily a bad thing. Now that I was on my own and around food constantly, I'd have to be careful not to make a habit of it.

While we were cooking, Austin popped through the doorway from the bar, a wide smile on his face. "Morning! I see you remembered how to turn on the fryer and get things going. You might not need me at all."

"You're right," Ronan said as he came from the walk-in. "We don't need you. Feel free to go enjoy your day off."

Though the words were nice, there was a possessive, almost grouchy undertone that I didn't quite understand.

I pressed my lips together and chose to ignore him altogether. "But while you're here, do you want some lunch? Ronan came in and showed me the books, and we were just getting ready to eat."

Tension crackled between the two men, and Ronan took a couple steps closer. "I'm sure he has other things to do."

I glanced back and forth between them. Though I didn't particularly care for Ronan's attitude, I also didn't know their history. I didn't want to step on the wrong side of any line, so I figured for now, it would be best to let it play out without interfering.

For a second, I thought Austin was gonna stand his ground, but then he smiled and dropped his gaze from

Ronan to me. "He's right. I need to go do some shopping, and then my friends are hitting the beach. I'll join them."

"Well, thank you for being willing to give up your day off for me," I said with a warm smile.

Austin's gaze had turned back to Ronan. "My pleasure. If you need anything at all, you have my cell."

He stuck his hands in the pockets of his neon-green board shorts, then turned and meandered back out the way he'd come.

I plucked the chicken patties out of the fryer basket with the tongs and placed them on the buns we'd prepared. "What was that all about?"

Ronan shook the fry basket in the hot oil, sending a hissing and popping of bubbles to the top. "What was all what about?"

I rolled my eyes. "Don't do that. I'm new, but I'm not stupid. There's obviously something between you two, and I don't want to deal with a power struggle, especially when I don't know its root."

He chuckled, but it had a tinge of arrogance. "Believe me, there's no power struggle. Austin knows his place, and I'm confident in mine. Everything is just fine."

I sighed but decided this wasn't a battle I needed to pick. At least not yet. If it continued to be an issue after I understood the dynamics, I'd address it then.

Since Austin and I had set up most of the bar the night before, we had plenty of time to eat.

"You know, you don't have to stick around the bar," he said, washing a bite of sandwich down with a swig of iced tea. "You just got here, and you have a lot going on in your head. Maybe you should take the day, put on your suit, and go enjoy the beach. Catch some rays. Read a book. In fact, you don't even have to go anywhere. You can do all that from right here."

He motioned toward the stretch of sand that led to the water, and I considered it. It was tempting to blow off everything and spend a day with my toes in the sand, but I felt like I needed to get up and running with the bar. Besides, I didn't really feel like my head was the best place to be right now, so keeping busy would be a good thing.

I lifted a shoulder as I dragged an onion ring through my puddle of ketchup. "I'll hang around for a little bit, at least. You can show me how to open the register and whatnot. The beach would be nice, though, so maybe I'll do that later this afternoon."

"Hey, you two!" a cheerful, familiar voice called. "Glad to see you both back today!"

Eddie gave me a quick sideways hug. "Girl, I was feelin' bad for you last night. You were runnin' your tail feathers off, and after drivin' eight hours, to boot. I hope you're takin' today off so you can sit on this side of the bar with us. You're one of the few people Cerbi actually enjoys."

I reached down and scratched the little guy's head, and he licked my hand. I resisted pulling away because he was so sweet, but after he'd licked me yesterday, my hand had smelled like something rotten. The little guy needed a doggy toothbrush. I smiled as he flipped over on his back for a belly scratch. I was definitely leaning toward getting a dog now that Rob and his infernal allergies were out of my life.

Erik gave Ronan the side-eye. "Since some people decided to show up to work after actin' like a five-year-old, you can relax today."

Ronan had the grace to blush, which surprised me for some reason. "All right. I get it. I was a jerk. And I've already told her to take the day off, so talk to her."

Though I wanted nothing more than to learn everything I could about the bar as quickly as I could, the other side of it was looking better and better the longer I sat down. So was the beach, for that matter.

"Maybe takin' the day off isn't a horrible idea," I said, and Erik and Eddie grinned.

Erik motioned for me to follow, and I did, leaving Ronan to do his thing. "Come sit with us. We'll show you how we pass a Thursday here in Florida."

I spent the next hour drinking with them while Ronan handled the slow but steady stream of customers. From what I'd learned from going over the books, we never really had dead days so, Lord willing, I'd be able to make a nice living here, and I'd do it all on my own.

Eddie was telling a lewd joke about a parrot, a pirate, and a priest when my phone rang. I pulled it from my pocket figuring it was one of the girls checking in or one of the boys wondering why I was summoning them. Instead, Rob's slimy face popped up on my screen. I declined the call, missing the days when I could pick up an actual receiver and slam it down again. Caller ID on a landline had been the best for making a point.

He called right back, and again, I declined it, tossing my phone on the bar in aggravation. When he did it again, I huffed out a breath and picked it up to silence it.

Eddie raised a brow. "You want me to take that, sugar?"

"Oh, let him," Erik exclaimed, an evil grin spreading across his face. "He'll make that man apologize to his mama for his own birth."

As much as the idea appealed to me, I didn't want to stoop that low. Well, I did, but I was trying to maintain the high road. Then it occurred to me that something might have happened to one of the boys. I scooped the phone up, took a deep, cleansing breath, and answered it.

"Jules, for the love of god, where are you?" he snapped when I said hello.

I stiffened. "Haven't you been to the house? I left you a note."

His tone was impatient and condescending and made me feel like he was chastising me like a kid who'd broken the rules. "What you left was one hell of a mess and some insanity scribbled on an electric bill. Seriously, when are you coming home? CiCi and Laurel aren't taking my calls, and even Marcus is giving me the cold shoulder."

"Gee, I wonder why?" I snarked, trying to keep a level tone even though my temper was hitting the boiling point. "You took advantage of him to get a good deal on your girlfriend's Porsche. As far as the mess, the one I made in our living room isn't a grain of sand compared to the one you made of our lives."

He went on like I hadn't even spoken. "Speaking of Marcus, I understand you bought a brand-new Mustang out of our savings?" He scoffed. "C'mon, Jules. That was just petty. Be reasonable—you're a little mature for muscle cars and spring breaks, don't you think? We have the boys to think of, and that money was for retirement. You can't just run off to Florida like some twenty-something with no responsibilities. You're almost fifty, for Christ's sake. Get back here and take care of business like an adult."

All the hateful things I'd thought of saying to him on my trip down here built within me, and the way he implied Bubbles—I spat her name in my mind—was perfectly deserving of a Porsche while I was too old for a sports car or a party ripped a wound in the fabric of my womanhood so wide that I hated him with every fiber of my being.

I tasted blood from where I was biting my tongue as he continued to drone on in that patronizing tone about how I needed to come back this instant to deal with property division, money, and divorce proceedings like an adult. The realization that I'd spent the best years of my life being who I was *supposed to be* rather than who I *was* in order to support this man built and tightened in my chest until I felt like I'd burst. Bitterness, resentment, betrayal, self-loathing —they all swirled inside me, creating what felt like a tempest that would surely kill me if I didn't release it. The edges of my vision had a red tint, and I knew if I didn't hang up, I'd spew all the poison in my heart right at him.

"Jules!" I heard Ronan call my name from a distance, and a disconnected part of me noticed that the weather had changed. Cerbi let out an eerie howl, and wind whipped my hair around my face. Bottles of liquor hovered midair, thunder boomed, and glasses exploded. "Jules, dammit, you have to calm down. Eddie, Erik, do something!"

Firm arms wrapped around me from either side, and with them came an intense feeling of peace that some part of my brain knew didn't belong to me. It stole over me, soothing the hurt and rage before everything went black.

Chapter Nine

"Jules." Somebody was patting my face, but I pushed them away, unwilling to retreat from the cottony-soft envelope of peace and safety cocooning me.

"Jules, wake up." This time, Ronan's voice was more firm and the pats turned to light slaps. "Guys, can you release her?"

"I think so." That was Erik, but his voice sounded so far away.

The warmth slipped away like somebody'd pulled a blanket off me, and Ronan said my name again.

"What?" I muttered, fluttering my eyes open. We were in my living room, and I was on the couch. Ronan knelt next to me, and Eddie and Erik peered at me over his shoulders.

"There you are," Ronan said, and I would have sworn I heard relief in his voice. "You had us worried."

"And mildly terrified before that," Erik said, his eyes wide as he examined me.

Eddie frowned at him and gave him a light smack on the arm. "Not helpful."

Erik's expression turned a little sheepish, but he shrugged. "Not untrue, either."

"What happened?" I asked, struggling to push to a seated position. My head felt like somebody'd dropped an anvil on it. I eased back onto my pillow as the room spun around me.

They glanced back and forth between each other, and I felt like I was missing some sort of silent conversation that my brain was still too mushy to follow. Apparently, though, poor Eddie drew the silent short straw. He scrunched his face up. "Well, Sweetie, you maybe sorta kinda caused just a teeny little hurricane-ish." He held his thumb and forefinger up with a half inch or so of space between them.

Erik rolled his eyes, "Oh, for the love of god, Eddie. Move." He squeezed around so he was close, then sat down on the edge of the couch beside me. "Jules, honey, what do you know about magic?"

A half-hysterical laugh bubbled up my throat. "Magic what? Mushrooms? Beans? Little green men? Unicorns fartin' rainbow glitter? Witches, wizards, evil sorceresses?"

Eddie nodded, but his expression, though a little wary, held zero humor. "All of that. Well, not the little green men. Those are aliens, sugar. And strictly speaking, magic beans and mushrooms aren't relevant to this particular conversation. But the rest, yeah. Witches, wizards, all that."

When their faces remained serious, the smile slid off my face, and I pinched my arm. Hard. Scowling, I rubbed the spot and shoved at Erik so I could sit up. The pain in my head had dulled to a low thrum, and once I was up, I propped my elbows on my knees and dropped my head in my hands for a minute.

I picked it back up. "Somebody start at the beginning, cuz y'all ain't makin' a lick of sense."

Ronan sat down beside me. "We weren't sure what you knew when you got here. Shit, we didn't even know you existed, but then I saw you wearing the necklace this morning, and I thought ... well, I didn't know what to think. You seemed oblivious to what it meant, but you could have been faking it."

I ran my tongue over my teeth and lowered my brows at him. "Somehow this doesn't feel like the beginning. I understand all the words but have no idea what they mean strung together like that."

Eddie rolled his eyes. "It's simple. Magic is real, sugar. Have you ever watched Supernatural or Harry Potter? They got a lot of things right, and if what you just did down there is any indication, you have a yacht load of it."

The warmth of Ronan's body transferred from his thigh to mine where we were touching. I instinctively reached for his forehead, probably because right now, mom genes were a safe space for my brain. "You're burning up. Are you fevered? Do you feel okay?" That would make a ton of sense. They were all fevered and hallucinating.

His full lips turned up into a wry smile. "I'm fine. That's one of the side effects, so to speak, of my particular brand of magic."

I thought about that for a second, then my mind drifted back to the wind and flying bottles down in the bar. I almost heard the click when my brain connected the raging tempest outside to the one that had been consuming me inside. The skies had been blue without so much as a single cloud when I'd answered my phone, and the bottles had been firmly grounded on the bar. Weather didn't change and inanimate objects didn't levitate on their own, and if I didn't believe anything else, I had faith in what I'd seen. One of my favorite Arthur Conan Doyle quotes sprung to mind—when you eliminate the impossible, whatever remains, no matter how improbable, must be the truth.

I whipped my head sideways so I was looking directly in Ronan's eyes. "Show me."

Erik's eyes rounded to the size of saucers. "Oh, I don't think that's a good idea. Baby steps, sweetie." He snapped his fingers, and a little flame appeared in his palm, flickering and dancing.

"So you're what—a witch? Warlock?"

He smiled. "Something like that, though wizard is the correct term for white magicals. Eddie and I both are, though we have different gifts. All magicals do. There are categories, but each gift is different. Unique."

"You're a wizard too?" I asked Ronan, still trying to wrap my head around things.

Eddie snorted. "He wishes."

Ronan arched a brow at him. "You wish you were as cool as me." He turned to me. "No, Jules. I'm a shifter. A wolf shifter to be exact."

I nodded, trying to keep an open mind. After all, hadn't I fantasized about just this sort of thing for most of my life. "So, you're a werewolf?"

He cringed. "That's one term, but I prefer shifter. I have total control over my change."

"Is that all the magic you have?" I asked.

Eddie giggled. "See? She's brand new, and even she's not impressed."

I scowled at him. "Be nice. I'm just trying to wrap my head around this without it exploding. Assuming you're not some pack of deranged lunatics, I think it's all cool. So what am I?"

Ronan sighed. "That's where things get a little tricky. We don't know your mother or what she might have been, but your father was a wizard, yes. Though like Erik said, if what we just saw is an example of what you can do when you don't even know you have powers, his magic didn't hold a candle to yours. We need to know your mom's history to get the total picture."

"That's easy. My mom was a social worker, and I can promise you she had no secret identity or super powers. She worked a nine-to-five job, made sure I got to band practice and Girl Scouts, and had an occasional girls' night out with her friends. She was spicy and loving and full of life, but I promise you, she wasn't magical."

Ronan pressed his lips together. "I'm not willing to just assume that, but you should probably talk to her about all of this."

Sadness washed through my heart, and I struggled to speak around the lump that had formed in my throat. "Believe me, with everything that's been going on, I'd like nothing better, but I lost her three years ago."

Ronan squeezed my knee, and sympathy radiated from him. "I'm sorry. Then let's skip to where you found the necklace. Did you find anything else with it? A leather book, maybe?"

I didn't know much about magic, but I did know enough that I now felt silly for not accepting the book for what it was. To be fair, though, nobody expects to find a real Book of Spells or grimoire or whatever, because, be serious.

I chewed my lip, not knowing whether or not I could trust these guys or not. My gut said yes, but I wasn't exactly on an even enough emotional keel to follow that blindly. Still, I had to trust somebody because apparently, I blew shit up and caused weather events when I lost my temper. I was probably gonna need some help getting a handle on that.

I nodded. "I did. Do you need me to get it?"

"It couldn't hurt," Ronan replied, so I pushed up from the couch.

"I'll be right back." I wasn't willing to show them where I'd found it yet. I squatted down to give Cerbi, who'd plunked down at the end of the couch, a rub and an apology. "Who's a good boy? What do you think of all this crazy, huh? Did Aunty Jules scare you earlier? I'm sorry."

"Ha!" Eddie barked. "Are you kidding? He was the only one of us who thoroughly enjoyed it! He thrives in chaos just like all hellhounds do."

I whipped my gaze toward the guys, incredulous, and nearly lost my balance in my squatting position. "Did you say hellhound?" I turned back to the adorable little puggle, then fell backwards square on my ass when, in Cerbi's place, a ginormous black dog with a lolling tongue and glowing red eyes now sat. He stood and stared down at me, then ran his rank-smelling tongue up the side of my face. At least now I understood why his breath smelled like dead possum.

"Knock it off, you oversized Pomeranian," I exclaimed, pushing the exuberant yet terrifying dog off me. "If you're an example of a hellhound, I have to wonder how much other stuff the movies got wrong,"

"Oh, they got a lot wrong," Eddie said. "But Cerbi isn't your average hellhound. He's actually more vicious than most in battle, but more importantly, he's smart. He likes going out with us, though, so he changes into something a little less intimidating. People are more willing to give fries and the last bite of cheeseburgers to a dog when they aren't terrified."

I pushed to a standing position, knees cracking. Cerbi

plopped down on his front legs, wagging his tail with his butt in the air.

"Yeah, okay," I said, rolling my eyes. "He looks horribly vicious. This is me running for my life."

I shuffled past him, wincing a little from the ache caused by squatting that long. I made a mental note to ask about an anti-aging spell, but I had a feeling it wasn't going to be that easy. My luck wasn't that good.

The reality of the situation slapped me in the face halfway to the bedroom, and the image of the little flame in Erik's hand popped to mind. I had to try something, and that seemed easy enough.

I held out my hand, envisioning the spark of fire in my hand. I wasn't sure what else to do, so when nothing happened, I doubled down on my intent. Fire shot from my hand straight to the ceiling, and I squealed then instinctively flicked my palm out away from my face. The fire shot to the filmy curtains, which burst into flame, then down across the tile.

"Oh, shit, oh shit, oh shit," I yelped, counterintuitively shaking my hand to put the fire out. By that point, the curtains, bed, and ceiling were aflame.

"Jules, stop! You're making it worse," Eddie barked as he ran into the room. Dodging the stream of flame, he grabbed my hand and closed his eyes. I sagged with relief when the flame went out, but the curtains and bed were still on fire.

Erik swept a hand toward the flame. "Vocare aquam!" Water spewed from his hand, and in just a couple seconds, my bedroom was a soaked, smoldering mess.

I pulled in a deep breath and blew it back out slowly, cursing myself for being stupid enough to try something that could have knocked me out of a home and a living at the same time. As it was, it was going to take me an entire day's work and a nice chunk of cash to fix what I'd destroyed. Or not. I rubbed my eyes when the water and scorch marks began to fade from the furniture, ceiling, and curtains until all signs of the madness were gone.

"What the hell?" I asked, staring around the room in amazement.

Ronan's lips curved into a smile. "I suspected as much when the place magically transformed from a quintessential man-cave to a modern beach home when you arrived, but I thought maybe you'd done it yourself."

"So, what?" I asked, my mind jumping to creepy things like the apartment watching me in the shower. "The place spies on me so it knows all my desires?"

Oh, boy. That could get interesting considering my attraction to Ronan. I coughed to cover a laugh when I pictured my apartment dragging him naked, kicking and screaming, to my bedroom at three a.m. Don't judge. A woman doesn't hit her peak until her forties, and that part of my life had been underwhelming for years.

Ronan tilted his head at me, his expression almost as salacious as my thoughts. I mentally froze in my tracks. What if he could read minds?

He smiled, which made me even more nervous. "I don't think your apartment is sentient in the way you think. I believe it's more that you're connected to it via your magic, and it's tuned to manifest your desires or needs."

I held up a hand. "Let's put a pin in that for now. As long as it's not creepin' on me in the shower, it's not a priority. How about we take a look at the book? I need to wash my face and recenter, so I'll be out in just a few. I'll meet you in the living room."

Erik held up a finger as he passed me. "No more magic unsupervised."

"Promise," I replied, sincere. I wasn't sure exactly how much my apartment could come back from, so I figured it was best to rein it in.

A couple minutes later, book in hand, I rejoined the guys on the sofa and balanced the book on my knees.

"The first time I looked at this, it was totally blank, which I thought was super weird. Then this morning, I checked it, and it just had one poem—or spell, I suppose—on the front page. The rest was still blank."

I flipped the book open and showed it to them.

"Oh boy," Erik said after leaning forward and reading it. "Did you happen to read this out loud? And were you wearing the necklace at the time?"

I nodded. "Yes to both. Why?"

Ronan ran his finger down the page, and I couldn't help but admire the elegant shape of his hand. It was hard to reconcile that part of him with being a wolf.

"This isn't a poem, honey. It's an awakening spell, meant to summon any dormant magic when in the presence of a talisman. Or at least in your case, that seems to be the process. It doesn't call for any sort of ritual, so I have to think it's the stone or the entire pendant that does it."

He flipped through a couple more pages, but the book remained blank.

"Now what do I do?" I asked, annoyed at the helplessness washing over me.

Eddie shrugged. "Now we start teaching you how not to blow shit—or people—up."

I gasped as my hand shot to my mouth. "I didn't—I mean, I was talking to Rob, and he made me *so* mad, and I was thinking horrible things about him."

Ronan laid his hand on my leg. "He's fine. Trust me, I made sure when I saw where you were headed. I told him you were busy and would return his call at your convenience."

"Yeah," Eddie said, grinning, "and with that sexy voice too. You may not have killed your ex, but I promise you he's dying of jealousy."

I scoffed. "I highly doubt that. You haven't seen Miss Perky Tits. Remember, he has a twenty-something girlfriend now. He's got no regrets, at least not yet."

Ronan's gaze traveled from my eyes and down my face and stopped at my cleavage, which I have to say looked pretty damned good in the blue tank top the ladies had bought me. He met my eyes with a look so scorching it nearly swallowed me whole. "Like I said before, no man in his right mind trades a woman for a girl. If he has no regrets, then that reflects on him, not you, Jules."

Be still my heart. My attraction to him grew about tenfold, not because of how he looked at me or what he said per se, but because I knew he wholeheartedly believed every word he'd just said. To my bruised and battered ego, that meant more than any pickup line or wolf-whistle—I smiled at the term—ever could.

"Phew," Eddie said, fanning himself. "Did it just get hot in here, or what?"

I smiled at him, grateful to him for breaking the tension, but at the same time wishing Ronan and I were alone. It had been a long time since I'd felt that pull, and I wasn't sure what to do with it. Scratch that. I knew exactly what I wanted to do with it, but now wasn't the time to jump a man just because he stroked my ego a little. I had enough issues.

"So," I said, clearing my throat and breaking eye contact. "What now?"

"Now your training starts," Erik said, then brushed off his hands.

"Nope," Ronan said. "First we have a drink. After today, I think we all need one. Since the bar's a hot mess, we can't reopen today anyway, so we may as well celebrate Jules's new powers with whiskey."

I cringed and held up a hand. Whiskey was my least favorite booze, and just the thought of it made me gag a little. "Make it a margarita, and I'm in."

If this wasn't a tequila kind of day, I didn't know what was. It struck me that I'd had a few of those back to back lately, but I decided to follow Scarlet O'Hara's lead and think about it tomorrow.

Chapter Ten

I couldn't believe the disaster I'd made of the bar. Most of the specialty glasses that had hung from racks above the liquor bottles were broken, and sand and glass were everywhere. Even the patio and barstools were a mess. It looked like a sandstorm had blown through the place.

"Holy shit," I said, mouth agape as I took in the damage. "I did all this?" A thought struck me so hard I almost stumbled. "What if there'd been people here? Are you sure nobody saw it?"

Ronan shook his head. "Nobody saw it. We got crazy lucky there, because that would have taken some creative storytelling to cover up. Don't think about what-ifs though. You have enough on your plate with reality right now."

He wouldn't get an argument from me, but there was one thing I *could* clearly check off my laundry list of crap things I had to do. "Hey, guys, I need to call my boys. I can't sit down and start planning a future with that still on my plate."

Ronan squeezed my hand. "It's gonna be okay."

I bit my lip. "I'm just not sure what to tell them. Do I just say we're getting a divorce, or do I tell them why? I don't want to be the bitter woman who tries to poison her kids against her ex."

Eddie patted my shoulder. "Be honest. They're not babies, and they deserve the truth. They'll sense if you're hiding something."

He was right. The boys had always been perceptive, and they deserved the truth. It wasn't my fault if that painted their father in an ugly light. I wavered for a second, dreading doing it. I'd have rather had my fingernails torn off, but I figured it was best to just do it and get it out of the way. Nothin' good ever came from sitting on bad news, and this one could blow up on me if I wasn't careful.

Even though I'd told them we'd talk this afternoon in my message, I took a chance and, moving to a table on the patio for some privacy, called them, hoping to catch them during lunch.

As I waited for them to pick up, I took a couple calming breaths—in through my nose, out through pursed lips. The boys and I had always been close, so I was less worried about negative or hateful responses than I was about the disruption I was about to cause to their lives.

Derek was the first to answer, but Bryan was only a few seconds behind him.

"Hey, mom! What's up?" Bryan asked. He was wearing his backpack and walking, and I could see a campus building behind him, though I didn't know which one it was.

I smiled, trying to project a calm I wasn't feeling. "Hey, baby. I have something I need to talk to you and your brother about. I'm not quite sure how to say it, but I wanted you to hear from me."

Derek chewed on his lip and sighed. I noticed he was having problems meeting my eyes. "You found out, didn't you?"

"Found out what?" Bryan asked. In some ways, I was glad at least one of them knew. I wasn't sure how, but I had no doubt from Derek's expression that this wasn't going to be news to him. At least not the cheating part. Honestly, I'd debated even telling them about that part. They'd still need to have a relationship with their father, and no matter what he'd done to me, Rob had always been a good dad. I didn't want to damage that for the boys' sakes.

Derek spoke before I could. "Dad's been having an affair."

I mashed my jaws together, trying not to let them see the huge crack that was running right down the middle of my heart.

Bryan stopped and took his backpack off, then sank down onto it. "What do you mean he's having an affair? That can't be right."

I nodded, trying to hold it together. "It is, baby. I'm sorry you had to find out this way."

He threw up the hand that wasn't holding the phone. "This way? What other way is there to find out? How did you find out? Are you okay?"

I tried to offer him a reassuring smile. "Your father told me. He wants a divorce, and to be honest, no, I'm really not okay. But I will be."

Derek remained silent, and the guilt etched across his face renewed my anger at Rob. "I'm sorry, Mom. I just didn't—"

Before I could say anything to comfort him, Bryan turned on him, anger and confusion warring for top expression. "You're sorry for what? That our dad was making a fool of our mom behind her back and you didn't tell her? How could you?"

I squeezed my eyes shut and took a deep breath. "Honey, you can't put this on your brother. He was in an impossible situation, and I'm sorry for that. That's not his fault—it's your father's."

I wasn't going to slander Rob, but I wasn't going to excuse his behavior, either.

Both boys were quiet for a minute, and I gave them that time to absorb the news. Lord knew I was having a hard enough time doing that myself, so I knew some of what they were feeling.

"You're leaving him, right?" Bryan asked after a few more heartbeats. "No way are you gonna forgive him for this. You deserve better than that."

Derek raised his gaze to mine. "Bryan's right, Mom. Don't forgive him. You gotta move out. I know it'll be hard, but please."

I guess that was as good an opening as I was going to get to tell them about my move. "About that. Remember the place your grandpa left me when he died?"

Bryan tilted his head. "You mean the one in Florida?"

I nodded. "Yeah. I might have behaved rashly, but the night your dad told me, I packed my clothes and moved here the next day. Yesterday, actually."

I watched the expressions flit across their faces. First confusion, then curiosity, then excitement. The last surprised me a little.

"Are you serious?" Derek asked, his dark eyes shining. "You really just moved to Florida and now you live there, and you own a bar?"

For the first time since the conversation had started, I smiled and meant it. "Yeah, that's exactly what I'm saying. I turned the phone and panned across the tiki bar and the beach beyond. "I guess this is home now."

Eddie and Erik waved to them from their stools on the bar.

"That's dope!" Bryan exclaimed, grinning. "When can we come and see you?"

I blew out a sigh of relief. This hadn't been the reaction I'd expected at all. "Anytime you want. Just let me know, and I'll buy the plane tickets. Just like when I was in Atlanta, and just like any other place I'll ever live, my house is your house."

"Dope!" Bryan exclaimed again. "Listen, I gotta go or else I'll be late for class." His expression turned serious. "Are you sure you're gonna be okay?"

I nodded. "I'm sure, baby. Go on to class, and if you wanna call me later, I'll be around."

He ended the call on his end, but Derek stayed on after he was gone. Tears of shame and anger glimmered in his eyes. "I'm really sorry, Mom. I saw them together a couple months ago, but I had no idea how to tell you. I just wanted to smash his face in. I was so angry for you, and I should've told you. Can you forgive me?"

I swiped a tear from my eye. "Oh, baby, there's nothing to forgive. You should have never been put in that position."

He gave me a watery smile. "You know I love you, right?"

I nodded through my tears. "Of course I do, and I love you too. To the moon and back."

He sniffed and smiled. "You might as well go ahead and buy our plane tickets down there now. In fact, don't wait until Thanksgiving. I know Bryan's the same as me. We want to see your new place as soon as possible. And of course, you're hosting our spring break. Havin' a mom who owns a bar on the Gulf of Mexico is gonna shoot Bryan's cool meter off the charts."

My heart swelled. This ugly conversation couldn't have gone any better. "Sure thing. We'll do another conference call in a couple days and see when you're both free. You're gonna love it."

We said our goodbyes, and I turned back to the bar, feeling about fifty pounds lighter. I hadn't realized how much the dread of that conversation had been weighing me down, but now that it was over, I felt for the first time like maybe things really would be okay. We'd find our new normal and move forward. Assuming, of course, I didn't accidentally blow the place up before they could see it.

One side of Ronan's mouth quirked up as I approach the bar. "I believe that's the happiest I've seen you look since you got here. I assume the conversation went well?"

I slid back onto my stool. "Better than I could've ever hoped. The boys are torqued about me livin' here, though I'm not sure how things are going to go with their father."

Eric lifted a careless shoulder. "That's his bed. He made it, now let him lie in it. It's no longer your problem."

Eddie bobbed his head as he took a sip of his beer. "Yep, sugar. That's his shit to shovel. Your horse don't even live in that barn anymore."

He held his glass up, and I clinked mine to his.

"New beginnings." Ronan tapped his bottle to mine as his gaze slid over me.

"New beginnings." I took a sip of the fresh drink he'd made for me while I was on the phone, then held it back to look at it. "What is this? It's absolutely delightful."

His eyes lit with pleasure. "It's called a pineapple fizz. A friend of mine gave me the recipe. Go easy on it because it has more rum in it than you'd think."

I nibbled on the pineapple wedge he'd put on the side of the glass. "I'm usually a margarita girl, but this just might convert me."

I glanced around the bar and was shocked to see that the mess I'd made was gone. There were only a few glasses hanging from the wooden racks, but the bottles were all back in their positions, and the broken glass and sand were gone.

"How on earth did you guys clean that up in the time it took me to make a phone call?" The place had been a disaster just fifteen minutes before.

Eric grinned and twinkled his fingers. "Sometimes having a little magic comes in handy."

I cocked a brow. "Sometimes? I sure hope that skill turns out to be in my wheelhouse. I'll never wash laundry or do dishes again."

He laughed. "Considering the two times you've used your magic, how about we hold off on getting fancy? I don't think learning magic is going to be your issue. I think we're gonna have a harder time teaching you to control it."

Cerbi, who'd stayed tight on my heels since we'd left the apartment, jumped up on my leg, begging for food. "I don't have anything, boy. I'm pretty sure you don't like pineapple rinds, and that's all I've got."

Ronan shook his head. "I've never seen him take to anybody like he has you. He usually just lays there and snoozes unless somebody offers him food. I think you've got yourself a friend."

I glanced at the now-clean bar, then at the three guys with me. "I think I've got more than one."

All things considered, I counted myself lucky. I already had friends, my boys didn't hate me, and I had magic. Not too shabby a start for my new life.

Chapter Eleven

Since the bar cleanup had been much easier than anticipated, Ronan went ahead and opened it up. I'd never been one for sitting on a bar stool all day, so I decided to put on my suit and spend some time on the beach. After the couple of days I'd had, a little ocean therapy and a good book sounded much better than drinking rum and drowning my sorrows.

Ronan volunteered to help me carry my stuff, but when I declined, he followed me off the deck and onto the sand. "At least let me carry a chair and an umbrella down for you."

He swerved to the right and scooped up one of the wooden loungers we kept there for guests who wanted to catch some rays without being too far from the bar. An umbrella leaned against the side of the building, and he grabbed it too. "No offense, but you don't look like you can take too much sunshine all at once."

I held my arm out and twisted it, noting that it still had a pink tinge from the day before. "Yeah, one of the pains of being a redhead."

His gaze traveled down the length of my arm and back

to my shoulder, then took in my green bathing suit top and bare midriff. If my arms hadn't been full, I'd have wrapped my arms around my not-so-tiny waist. Cici and Laurel had slipped some suits into the stuff they'd bought me, and this one was the most modest in the bunch. I planned to give them an earful about that the first chance I got, but for today, it was this or a tank top and shorts.

His gaze returned to my face. "You should be proud of how you look. It's how the goddess made you." His lips curled up into a sexy smile. "And believe me, she outdid herself."

I rolled my eyes and nudged him with my elbow. "You're something else, you know that? I know we got off to a rough start, but I really look forward to getting to know you better."

Warmth spread from my elbow and up my arm, and I wondered if he felt the same thing I did every time we touched. I shook my head. I'd just found out a couple of days ago that my husband of twenty years was cheating on me, and now here I was, having these sorts of thoughts for another man like some teenage horn-dog. I needed to pump the brakes because I had a feeling this man was going to be in my life for a long time. Whatever relationship I built with him, I wanted it to be a strong one. If that was friendship, then I didn't want to mess that up by bringing ill-fated romance or meaningless sex into it. If it was going to be romance, I didn't want to jump into it before my messed up emotions had settled into their new normal. That didn't mean I couldn't enjoy the eye candy, as Cici and Laurel would have put it. The way his work T-shirt fit him should have been illegal. The man was jacked. He had to have been at least six-four, and if his arms, shoulders, or back had an ounce of fat on them, I sure couldn't see it. I resisted the urge to run my fingers over his tattoos.

"Feel free to tell me it's not my business, but are all your tattoos just for looks, or do they mean something? My experience with magic is limited to what I've seen on TV and in the voodoo shops I saw in New Orleans, but they look like runes of some sort."

He glanced sideways at me as we trudged through the sand. Or rather, I trudged. He looked perfectly at ease. "They are runes of a sort. They have a story and a purpose, but that's for another day."

We'd arrived at a spot just above the tide line. "Do you want to be up here, or would you rather I sat the chair down at the edge of the water where you can dip your feet in? The only problem with doing that is that the waves coming in and out will pull the sand from underneath of you, and you'll sink. You'll have to move it every few minutes."

I laughed. "That sounds like a lot of work. I just wanna sit and read my book and relax. Here will be fine. I can get up and walk down to the water to cool off." Since it was hotter than a griddle at a pancake joint, I figured that would be often.

He plopped the lounger down, then stabbed the umbrella into the sand and opened it for me. "Give me your sunscreen. I'll put some on your back because if you miss any spots, you'll blister for sure."

I fished through my bag and pulled it out, then handed it to him and turned around so he could put it on. Goosebumps ran up my arms in anticipation, and I shook my head. This was in direct opposition to what I'd just been thinking, but I couldn't dispute the logic. I rounded my shoulders a little without being too obvious, trying to smooth out the love handles and the places where the flab bulged over my strap. It wasn't out of control, but I'd had two kids and hadn't exactly been a gym rat the last twenty years.

He was nice enough to warm the lotion up between his hands before he rubbed it on.

This is not an insanely hot man who can turn into a wolf rubbing you down, Jules, I told myself. *It's a friend making sure you don't get a sunburn.*

No matter how many times I repeated that to myself, it didn't stop the warmth that was spreading through my belly. When he increased the pressure at my shoulders and pushed his thumbs into muscles that had been tense for days, it was all I could do not to groan.

"You should book yourself a massage," he said, his voice husky. "We have several good therapists I could recommend."

He ran his hands over my back one final time to rub the lotion in, then squeezed my shoulder. "Enjoy your day."

Before I could say anything else, he turned and strode up the beach. I swallowed hard. I hadn't even felt attraction like that for Rob when we'd been all hands and hormones in college, and I wasn't quite sure what to do with it.

After a few seconds, my heart slowed back to a steady rhythm, and I pulled my book from my bag. It took me almost a full chapter to whip my wonky libido back into place, but then I lost myself in the world of witches, faes, and other magical beings. The fact that I was now part of that world wasn't lost on me, but I wasn't willing to give up my guilty pleasure just because it had become my new reality. Also, it wasn't like I was fighting evil wizards to save humanity. I was just trying to get through the day without burning down my own house.

I'd just gotten back from taking a dip in the water to

cool off when my phone rang. Hunkering under the umbrella so I could see the screen, I dried my face as I took the group call.

"So tell us everything," CiCi said, her eyes lit with excitement. "Oh my god—you're at the beach! Spill—we want to hear about every second you've been there!"

A bubble of semi-hysterical laughter nearly escaped my throat before I caught myself. I could just imagine how *that* conversation would go. *Everything is just great. I found out I'm a witch by causing a sandstorm in my bar, the hot bartender I told you about is actually a wolf shifter, and I almost burned my house down trying to light a fire in my palm.*

Yeah, that probably wasn't the way to start the conversation. I'd figure out how much, if anything, to tell them later, but first I need to figure it out for myself. I felt a little guilty and isolated, because these women knew everything about me, and I'd never hidden anything from them. Like I'd done with so many things lately, I pushed that to the back of my mind and made it a problem for future me.

I spent the next half-hour telling them about everything that had gone on at the bar that wasn't related to magic, then they filled me in on all the juicy stuff I'd missed in two days. Oddly, gossip that would have had me leaning forward on my elbows in interest a week ago now seemed trivial. It did ground me, though, because it brought a little bit of normalcy to my life.

Once they'd told the last tale, I panned my phone to show them where I was at.

"You know we hate you a little bit right now, right?" Laurel asked, one brow raised. "When can we come see you?"

As badly as I wanted to see the two people who knew

me best, I figured it would probably be better to wait until I knew I wouldn't hurt them or expose magic. Actually, I wasn't even sure what the rules were there, but it was common sense that if I'd lived my forty-nine years without seeing a unicorn or a werewolf—excuse me, shifter—then there was a decent chance that I wasn't supposed to tell anybody.

"Let me get settled," I said, pushing the mental quandary aside. "There's a lot I need to learn about the bar, and we're short staffed, so I'll probably be working a lot too."

I felt a little stab of guilt for making up that last part.

CiCi rolled her eyes. "Fine, but we're only giving you two weeks. Then we're gonna show up whether you want us to or not."

I grinned. "Deal."

Surely I could learn the rules and get my magic well enough in hand to avoid disaster for at least a weekend. "I can't wait to see you both."

Despite reapplying my sunscreen twice, I was starting to feel a little crispy three hours later. I was also thirsty enough to spit dirt and wished I'd brought more than one bottle of water with me. I wouldn't be making that mistake again.

I gathered my book and my towel and stuffed them in my bag, then cranked the umbrella down. I blew out an annoyed breath when I stared at the football field of sugar sand between me and the bar. It was going to be a long trip hauling the chair and the umbrella back up, but I didn't want to leave them on the beach because somebody would surely steal them. I'd just wrangled the umbrella out of the sand and onto my shoulder when Ronan appeared beside me.

"Here, I'll get that." He plucked the umbrella out of my

hands and stuffed it under his arm like it was no more awkward than a newspaper, then leaned over and deftly flipped the chair over so that he could pick it up too.

"Thanks. I'm not gonna lie—I wasn't looking forward to toting this all back up there by myself." No need to play the heroine because he'd see through that quickly enough. I wasn't lazy, but I did pride myself on being efficient. Plus, if I was honest, I was glad to see him again.

He adjusted his stride to mine as we moved toward the bar and looked at me sideways. "Did you have a good afternoon? You look relaxed, and you're barely even pink except for your cheeks."

I smiled. "As a matter fact, I did. And thanks for helping with the sunscreen and everything else. You need any help around the bar?"

He shook his head. "Nope. I'm all set. There's some stuff I want to show you, but it can wait. You had a big day, and you deserve some relaxation. Unless I miss my guess, your apartment is probably set up with all of your favorite movies and streaming channels. Grab a shower, order a pizza, and chill, as the kids say."

His gorgeous lips curled into a teasing smile, and for the first time in a long time, I followed my impulse instead of my common sense. "I have a better idea. Why don't you join me? You can fill me in a little more on the magical stuff. I'll still order pizza, but it'd be nice to have some company."

He opened his mouth to say something, then snapped it shut. We made it almost back to the bar by the time he spoke. "I have some things to do, so I'm afraid I'll have to take a rain check."

I did my best to offer him a genuine smile. "Sure thing. I should probably get some rest anyway."

I tried not to let that sting, but my cheeks got hot. This

was one of the first times in my life I was actually grateful to have a little bit of a sunburn. I gave myself a mental forehead slap—what had I been thinking?

I shook my head. That didn't feel right to me. I know I'd been out of the game for twenty years, but I was pretty sure mutual sexual attraction hadn't changed in that span of time. I wasn't imagining the smoldering gazes or the heat that traveled between us whenever we touched, so I scowled and shoved all the self-doubt out of my head.

Maybe he didn't want to get mixed up with a woman who had kids, or maybe I was just too much of a hot mess right now. I was also his boss, so that might have been playing a part. I reminded myself that regardless of what it was, I should be grateful for it. There was no doubt in my mind that my marriage was over, but that didn't mean I was ready to jump straight into another relationship.

Something in my gut told me Ronan was worth way more than rebound sex, but I wasn't even ready to think about that much yet. Or so I told myself as I peeled my eyes away from how his back rippled under his shirt when he set the lounge chair down in the sand. Just because he was out of bounds didn't mean I was blind.

Chapter Twelve

It was at least fifteen degrees cooler under the shade of the tiki bar, and Ronan had the ceiling fans as well as these strange air misters circulating air. I hung my beach bag off the hook under the bar and slid onto a stool. The guys were already gone, so I pulled out my phone and opened up my Pokémon app. I spent a few minutes playing with it while Ronan made me another one of those yummy rum drinks.

He smiled as he slid it across the counter along with a glass of ice water. "I made this one a little lighter. Until you get used to the sun and the heat, you might want to take it a little easy on the booze and double up on your water. Drinking's an entirely different beast here."

I pulled the glass of water toward me and drained half of it before I even took a sip of the pineapple fizz. "As crazy thirsty as I am, I don't think that's gonna be a problem."

"He's a wise man," a feminine voice laced with humor said from behind me. "Listen to him."

A blonde woman about my age slid onto a stool a couple

down from mine, smoothing the edges of her flowered yellow sundress.

"Hey, Janelle," Ronan said, sliding a draft beer in front of her. Apparently, he knew her well enough to remember what she drank, so I assumed she was a regular.

He turned to her. "Janelle, I'd like you to meet Jules. She's the new owner of the Flamingo. Jules, this is Janelle. You'll be seeing her quite a bit."

I pivoted my stool toward her and smiled. "Nice to meet you. Do you live around here?"

Janelle nodded and pushed her hair over her shoulder. "Yeah, I moved down here three years ago from Maine. I hated the winters, and when my husband took off with another woman, I was ready for a change of scenery. I figured I might as well go somewhere warm."

She took a drink of her beer and shook her head. "I was so pissed and hurt that I just slid my finger down the coast of Florida until I found the name of a town I liked, threw my stuff in a car, and never looked back. We didn't have any kids, so it wasn't like I was tied to the place."

I raise my brows. "Wow! You basically just told my story, except for the kid part. I have two boys in college. Was her name, by any chance, Bubbles?"

Janelle barked out a laugh, her brown eyes sparkling. "Bubbles? Oh, you poor girl. Mine left with Charise. At least yours makes your ex sound like a moron. Come on down, and let's exchange war stories."

I moved down a stool and spent the next two hours ex-husband-bashing and discussing the benefits of living in a small, coastal town. It was encouraging that she loved Dolphin Key, and I couldn't wait to do some of the stuff she told me about.

She finished off her last beer. "I'm doing a wine-and-painting class day after tomorrow. You should go with me. It's down at the Cranky Conch at seven."

I tilted my head. "A wine-and-painting class? I used to love to paint, and I love a good red. Is the title pretty much self-explanatory?"

She grinned. "It is, and if you enjoy both, then this is right up your alley. Honestly, you don't even really need any painting skills. I just go for the socialization, though I do have some cute pieces I've painted at other ones."

She gave me directions to the Cranky Conch, and we made plans to meet there a half hour early so we could eat.

"I have to go now, but I'll see you then." She paid her tab and left.

Ronan refilled my water glass when she was gone. Everybody had cleared out but him and me. "Looks like you made a new friend. She comes in here once or twice a week. I don't know much about her, but she's always nice. She's also always alone, so it might be good for you to get to know each other."

I swirled my straw in my drink. "Yeah, maybe so. I have two best friends at home. We've known each other since college, and they're a big part of my life." I met his eyes. "No offense, but it might be nice to keep one part of my life normal, at least. I have a feeling things are gonna get a little crazy, so maybe that'll help keep me grounded."

He reached across the bar and laid his hand over mine. "I know it has to sound nuts to you right now. I can't even pretend to imagine what you're going through, finding out about magic at this point in your life. I was born into it, so it's part of the fabric of who I am. I can't imagine anything else. Here you are, though, dealing with so many other things, and now this. I promise you that your life isn't going to change as much as you think it will. Or at least, who you are won't change." He winked at me. "What you can *do* will, though. Just wait until you don't have to wash dishes."

I smiled, and the runes on his arm caught my attention when he pivoted sideways to put glasses in the freezer. "When are you gonna tell me the story behind the tattoos? Now that you've framed it in such a mysterious way, I'm about to die from curiosity."

He glanced at me sideways, a lazy smile curving his lips. "You know what they say about curiosity and the cat."

I laughed. "I'm okay with it since I'm not a cat." I paused and raised a brow, thinking of Professor McGonagall from Harry Potter, who could transfigure into a cat. "Or am I?"

He chuckled. "Not that I'm aware of. Being a shifter is a little different than being a witch. That's not something you would've been unaware of for forty-nine years."

I pressed my lips together and nodded, trying not to giggle. "Yeah, I suppose I would've noticed the litter box, though I do have to say middle age has brought a few whiskers."

I closed my eyes as heat traveled to my cheeks. I'd just made a chin-hair joke to one of the most beautiful men I'd ever slapped eyes on.

I needn't have been embarrassed because he snickered. "You don't have to tell me about whiskers, remember? As I was growing up and learning to control my shift, I missed those more than once. It took me a full year to master it. My sisters thought it was hilarious and told all of their friends."

I tried to keep a straight face, but when I pictured him with whiskers, I almost spit my drink out. "You're making that up!"

He held up his hand. "Right hand to gods. They still tease me about it to this day."

I wasn't sure if he was being honest or if he was just

trying to make me feel better because he knew I'd embarrassed myself with the chin-hair reference, but I had a feeling he wasn't the type of person to make things up no matter what the reason. Also, the whiskered image of him forever burned in my brain made him a little more human to me. It was hard to relate to somebody that looked like the statue of a Greek god, so adding some fluffy whiskers to the image did a lot to bring him off his pedestal.

The grin faded from his face as he studied me for a second. "Is that invitation for dinner and a movie still open if we change it to tomorrow night?"

I pulled a twenty from my purse and slid it across the bar as I finished off my drink. "As long as you're not gonna make me watch a Western or musical."

His eyes lit with mischief as he slid the bill back across the bar. "Deal. I'll bring the wine. And your money's no good here."

I huffed and shoved it back toward him. "Don't be ridiculous. You're just like the rest of us and have bills to pay, and this *is* your job after all. I'm not gonna pay for the booze, but I will pay for your time."

He plucked it off the bar, smirking. "You're the boss."

I scooped my beach bag off its hook and headed around the bar toward the stairs that led to my apartment. All in all, the day had ended much better than it had started.

It turned out to be a good thing Ronan had skipped hanging out with me because by the time I made it up the stairs, the excitement and lack of sleep over the last couple days caught up with me.

I jumped in the shower to hose the saltwater and sweat off, but the pull of the Jacuzzi tub was too much to resist. I dimmed the lights, lit the citrus-bergamot candles that apparently my house had been kind enough to provide, and tossed in a lavender bath bomb that I'd brought with me. The only thing missing was a glass of wine and a book, so once I had those, I was set. The low lighting and candles provided just enough illumination to read, and I stayed in there with the jets massaging my back until I started to prune. Oddly, the water never got cold. I could get used to this whole magic thing.

It was still early when I got out, so I knew if I went to bed then, I'd be up at four o'clock in the morning. I was an early riser, but that was too early even for me. Instead, I made myself a cup of tea and took it to my deck for my first official thankfully–parrot–free Florida sunset. I had a score to settle with that old bird, but I didn't want to do it while I was relaxing.

Chapter Thirteen

Since I'd learned my house had basically remodeled itself for me, I was confident that the sheets were fresh. I was a little embarrassed by how excited I was to sleep under that silly Sherpa blanket. I'd always wanted one, but Rob had complained that he didn't like how it felt, plus it really didn't match the more formal decor of my bedroom.

Thinking back, that probably should've been a sign. They always say your bedroom should be the place where you're most comfortable and relaxed. It's not that I'd hated my bedroom. It was just that, like the rest of the house, I'd skipped a lot of the personal touches that would've clashed with the modern style. I looked around and gave a shuddery little squeal when I realized this room and this house were mine to do with as I pleased. No executives to impress and no husband I had to share my tastes with.

I didn't realize until I was already in bed that one of my socks had missed the hamper. Not wanting to leave the softness of my bed, I bit my lip and debated. I could just ignore it, but it was so out of place in the neat room that it bugged me. I tried to think of any way a flying sock could damage my house but came up with nothing.

Tentatively, I tried to do what all the heroines in my books did–I reached inside of me and tried to find my magic. Weirdly, I did, or at least I found something that was strange and a little buzzy. I pointed toward the sock, and wiggled my finger just a bit, willing it to lift from the floor. I got so excited when it actually did that I got cocky and waved my hand toward the basket, going for a bank shot. Instead, it shot sideways with such momentum that it actually knocked a hole in the drywall. I jumped to my feet to examine the damage and reached for the sock. Before I could pull it from the hole, though, the wall healed around it, leaving it hanging there, dangling like a pink-and-blue-striped tongue.

I rolled my head on my shoulders and heaved a big sigh. "Really? You couldn't wait for me to pull the sock out of the hole before you fixed yourself?"

I flapped my hand at it, careful not to infuse any magic, and climbed back into bed. In the scheme of things, extricating a sock from the drywall didn't even make my top-fifty list of things to do.

I snuggled back into my bed, loving the soft feel of the blanket and the crisp feel of the pink Egyptian cotton sheets. The last thing I thought as my eyes drifted shut was that I could get used to living like this.

I slept like a rock all night, not even getting up for a trip to the bathroom, and when I woke up the next morning I felt better than I had in a long time. Sure, I was still stiff, but I was relaxed and more well-rested than I'd been in forever. I made it through the morning without having to fight that stupid bird, though to be fair, I was a little disappointed he hadn't shown up. So far, it was bird – one, me – nothing, and I wasn't satisfied with that score.

I'd slept later than I usually did even though I'd gone to bed early, so the sun was up, and people were already at the beach while I was having my second cup of coffee. While I debated what to do that day, my mind drifted to the safety deposit box key. I'd made a note of what bank we use, so solving that mystery went to the top of my list. I needed to open up a checking account anyway, so I'd kill two birds with one stone.

I was pleasantly surprised to find there was no line at the bank. In Atlanta, going to the bank was a chore, which is why I did everything online when I could. When I stepped to the counter, I told the teller who I was, and she summoned a manager to take me back to the vault.

"Your dad was a good customer here for many years," the aging bald man told me as he motioned me into the room. "I hope we can keep your business now that he's gone."

He showed me which box was mine, then left the room. Taking a deep breath, I slid the key into the lock. I hesitated for a second because right now it was a mystery. Once I swung it open, I was either going to be excited or disappointed, and frankly, I wasn't sure which to wish for. I'd had plenty of excitement to last me for a while, but I kinda wanted to find something cool too. The box was a smaller one, and when I swung the lid open, I wasn't sure how to feel when the first thing I saw was an envelope with my name on it. I slid my finger under the flap and broke the seal, then pulled out a sheet of lined paper with a handwritten letter.

My dearest Jules,

I know you must hate me for leaving you and your mother, but believe me when I tell you I only did it for your safety. I don't know how much you know about yourself and me yet, and I don't want to put it in writing. It's not safe. Instead, look to the book and talk to Ronan. He knows the entire story, and you can trust him. That can't be said for most people, though, so always watch your back and remember that things are not always as they seem.

In this box, you'll find some savings bonds that I bought over the years for the boys. Yes, I'm well aware that I have two magnificent grandsons, and you have no idea how much it's broken my heart not to be a part of their lives. It's been almost as awful as not being a part of yours. Still, if I had it to do all over again, I would. You've lived and thrived, and so have they, and that's all I've ever wanted. I can't say that would have been the case had I stayed around.

I'm sorry to leave you such a cryptic message, but putting anything other than this little bit of information in black and white could harm many more people than just you and me.

I will take just a second to say this as a father—you're too good for the man you married. I've followed him just as I followed you, and he doesn't deserve you.

I swiped a tear from under my eye and scoffed. Apparently, I was the only adult on the planet the jackass had fooled.

As of this writing, bad things are coming. I hope I have the strength to face them and defeat them, but if you're reading this, I didn't. I've left you the bar and the apartment so you have an income and a safe space, but please don't let your guard down.

May the goddess watch over you and give you the power to succeed. I'm sorry I failed and left the fate of so many people in your hands. That's a huge burden to carry and one that I never wished on you. Good luck, and I love you more than you could ever know.

Yours always,
  Dad

PS Be careful. The dreadful beast you'll think is a parrot bites.

I laughed at that through my tears even though it didn't entirely make sense. I refolded the letter and stuffed it back in the envelope, then stuck it in my purse. True to his word, there were enough savings bonds to pay for the boys' college and then some.

The other two items confused me a little. One was the ring that matched my necklace that he'd been wearing in all the pictures in the album, and the other was a birth certificate for a woman named Delilah Charlotte Stone. Her mother was listed as Margaret Ann Stone, but there was no father listed. The woman had been born a full decade after I had, which sent all types of questions spinning through my head.

I dug through the box hoping I'd missed something, but there was nothing else. I took a picture of the birth certificate with my phone, then placed it and the savings bonds back in the box. I put the ring in a zipper pocket in my purse, then stashed the safety deposit box back in the wall and locked it.

Despite my intention to open a checking account, my

mind was too full to focus on something so mundane. I waved to the bank manager and thanked him on my way out, but that's about all the presence of mind I had.

It looked like the only person who could give me the answers I sought was coming for pizza and a movie that night. Now all I had to do was wait.

Chapter Fourteen

"All I'm saying is that he said to ask you."

Ronan had shown up ten minutes ago, and I might've been a little hasty when I'd asked for answers. In fact, the poor man had barely gotten through the door before I dive-bombed him.

He rubbed the bridge of his nose. "And I'd be more than happy to answer any questions you have, but you need to ask one first. I mean, all you told me is that you found his ring, a birth certificate, and a letter. I haven't even seen that yet."

I blew a breath out, puffing my cheeks in frustration as I paced my kitchen. "That's just it. I don't know what questions to ask. How about this? Were you and Dad working on anything? Like, is there some big bad witch or something out there trying to take over the world? Was somebody trying to kill him?"

He sighed and took a seat at the counter. "I think it's time to start at the beginning. I hadn't really planned to drag you to the deep end before you even knew there was a pool, but that seems to be where we're at. Can we at least order food first? I haven't eaten."

I popped the cork out of the bottle of wine he'd brought and poured us each a glass. "Already done. It should be here in ten minutes or so."

He furrowed his brow. "How do you know what I like on my pizza? How do you know if I have any allergies or not? No offense, but that was kind of rude."

In fairness, those were legitimate questions, and it was definitely a little rude, or at least it would have been had I not somehow known in my bones exactly what he liked. I lifted my shoulder. "All the meats plus mushrooms and green peppers."

He narrowed his eyes. "Who told you that?"

"Nobody." I slid his glass of wine across to him. "I just thought about you when I was ordering the pizza, and it popped into my head. Kind of an overreaction, though, don't you think? We're talking pizza toppings, not nuclear codes."

He studied me for a moment, suspicion plain on his face. "What am I thinking right now?"

I stared into his eyes, but it occurred to me that I probably didn't want to try using magic on somebody's brain. I took an educated guess instead. "You're thinking how soothing it would be to strangle me."

His lips quirked, and I knew I almost had him.

"C'mon. You've seen what's happened the two times I've used my magic. You really want me to try to crawl around in your melon with that grenade? I just knew, okay? But to answer your question, no, I don't know what you're thinking right now."

Apparently satisfied that I wasn't plucking random thoughts out of the air, he took a sip of his Merlot. "It could just be that you're intuitive. Your dad sure was. Sometimes all we had to do to get an answer to a question was ask it."

I took a seat on the bar stool next to him. "I don't understand."

"Just like you did with the pizza." He turned his hand palm upward. "You wondered what I liked on mine, and then you knew. I've never met anybody with that particular gift, but maybe you inherited it from him."

Since reading the letter, I was looking at my dad in a whole new light, and the idea of sharing traits with him brought him a little closer to me. "What else could he do? No, wait. I feel like that's starting at the end rather than the beginning. Or at least the middle. Let's start with where you two met."

He smiled. "I can answer that, but it's probably going to freak you out a little."

I rolled my eyes. "Yeah, because I haven't been idling at *freaked out* for three days already."

"Fair enough. I met your dad in a little pub in Ireland back in the eighties."

"In the eighties?" I scratched my eyebrow, trying to do the math on that. "Okay, color me intrigued, but I'm not quite freaked out yet. So you met him as a kid, so what?"

He laughed as he swirled his glass on the marble countertop. "No, this is where the freak-out part starts. I was a full-grown man. Shifters don't age quite like humans do."

Deciding to unpack that one later, I held up my finger. "Ah, that brings me to another question. This one's not exactly in line with what we're talking about, but let's call it a bonus. Am I a human?"

He scrunched his face up and wobbled his hand from side to side. "Yes and no. Biologically, you're mostly human, but somewhere in your background, you're not. At some point, one of your ancestors had a baby with fae. Or, if you prefer to look at it the other way, one of your fae ancestors had a baby with a human. That's why I was so curious about your mother."

Now that made more sense. "I've actually been thinking about that too. I've had a lot to think about all day, in fact. I can promise you beyond a shadow of a doubt that my mother was one-hundred-percent human. Not because I don't think she could have been magical, but because my grandmother was one of the meanest people God ever stretched hide over. If she'd had any magic at all, there would've been a path of destruction and dead bodies a mile wide behind her. My grandfather, bless his heart, would've probably been one of her first victims."

He laughed. "Okay, since that's a dead end anyway, we'll go on that assumption. That leaves your dad's lineage. I already happen to know that he has a long pedigree of powerful magic in his background, so you wouldn't have necessarily needed to get anything from your mother."

That was problematic for me because I didn't know anything about anybody on my father's side. I didn't even know my grandparents' names or where they were from or anything. I said as much.

"I don't know a whole lot of the details, either," he replied. "My mother might be able to help you if you really want the answers, but for practical purposes, the information isn't really relevant right now. Magic is subjective and unique, and just because your grandparents or your father, or anybody else in your family line, could do something doesn't mean that you'll be able to. On the flip side, you might have gifts that nobody in your family has previously had. It didn't used to be that way, but as the world has gotten smaller and magical people have intermingled, things have changed."

I thought about that, and it made a certain sort of sense. You saw it in the human world too. Four siblings could be completely different. One could be a basketball star, one could be a rocket scientist, one could be a musician, and the other could be a veterinarian.

I flipped the conversation back to something that mattered. "Back to how you and my father met. If it was in the eighties, I was still little, so it was probably shortly after he left us."

His face clouded with a hint of the sadness that filled my heart. "That makes a lot of sense. When I met your dad, he wasn't in a good place. I thought maybe somebody he loved had died, but if he walked away from his family, it probably felt even worse to him than that. He was a good man."

I pressed my lips together and tried to swallow the lump in my throat. "Do you know why he left us?"

One side of his mouth curved up into a kind half-smile. "I can guess. The magical world faced a huge threat, and your father was the only person in a position to restore the balance of power. Since you were a child, it would have been bad had anybody known you existed."

I stood up and paced, unable to sit still while I processed all of this. "You're telling me that of all the magical people in the world, my dad was the only possible option?"

He nodded. "Unfortunately, that's exactly what I'm saying. You see, your family has a very specific skill set, and I'm afraid you're the last in the line."

My mind immediately went to my boys, and a burst of fear shot through my heart.

He held up a hand. "I know what you're thinking, but your kids aren't in any danger. If they were girls, we'd be having an entirely different conversation, but since they're boys, you have nothing to worry about."

"What does that even mean?" I rubbed the back of my neck, trying to puzzle it out for myself but failing.

"What you need to understand is that many magical bloodlines are passed through the woman, and it's not uncommon for them to be stronger than the males. In fact, that's exactly the case with you and your father. He was trying to continue the responsibilities of your family line, but it's a female position. He did a damned good job of it, but he struggled. He didn't have the power necessary, so he formed alliances that helped offset that. That's the real reason we met. He needed somebody in the shifter community that he could trust because things were ugly. He managed to bring the balance back, but just barely."

Things were starting to click into place. "I'm gonna need you to expound on that a bit, but I'm beginning to think my father didn't abandon me. He saved my life."

He lifted a shoulder. "I knew your father probably better than anybody did, and I can promise you that whatever his reasons were for leaving you, it wasn't because he didn't want you. He just wasn't that type of a man. In many ways, I felt sorry for him because I figured out long ago that he kept relationships superficial, not because he didn't want to be close to anybody, but because he didn't want to put them in danger."

I rubbed my temples as I paced. "How, exactly, would he have put them in danger? I mean, what is this family responsibility you're talking about?"

"That's probably the best place to start, actually. There isn't really a good English translation for the title, but the closest it gets is the Mistress of Harmony. Or Balance, maybe."

Before he could continue, the doorbell rang. About the only annoying thing about the apartment was that there was no direct exit out the front. I scowled. "Whoever designed this place was an idiot. I'll be right back."

He grinned. "Maybe they were a tactical genius. Has it occurred to you how unsecure a staircase that leads into a public parking lot could be? Right now, you're hidden in plain sight. From the outside, there's no real indication that this is an apartment. Stay put. I'll go get it."

I suppose he was right when I looked at it like that, but it didn't make it any less irritating that I couldn't get pizza delivered right to my door. A few minutes later, we regrouped in my living room with the pizza and the bottle of wine on the coffee table.

"Okay, you were telling me about the whole harmony/balance thing. Let's pick back up there." I took a big bite of my pizza and chewed while I waited for him.

He peeled open the little container of garlic butter and shook his head, smiling. "You're very like him, you know. He was impetuous and kind and single-minded. He could out stubborn any mule, but he was diplomatic enough to make the poor animal feel good about giving in. That's why he was so good at carrying out your family's duties. He was also funny and smart, but he carried a sadness that you don't have. Now I know why."

After he said so many nice things, I hated to use the one semi-negative trait he mentioned, but I was dying to know the rest of the story. I turned, instead, to the diplomacy. "If you'd like to finish your pizza before we continue, that's fine."

I really hoped he wasn't going to take me up on that, but I did feel bad for rushing him while he was trying to eat.

He waved his slice. "Good try, but I know you're about to vibrate out of your skin with curiosity. I've only known you a couple of days, but I'm already coming to understand that patience is not necessarily one of your virtues."

I grinned. "Then please, continue posthaste."

"I figured you'd say that. I assume you know about the Dark Ages?" When I nodded, he continued. "Humans call it that because there wasn't much cultural or social development that took place during that time. What they don't know is why. Magic was in a serious state of flux at that point. Dark wizards were summoning demons and forming alliances with each other in order to exterminate good magic. They almost did it too. They were devious and figured out that even though they couldn't defeat entire covens or entire peoples, they could pick them off one at a time. It came to a point where there wasn't much good magic left. There were clusters and pockets, but it no longer flourished."

He was sitting on one end of the couch, and I was sitting on the other, so I pivoted so that I was facing him with my leg on the couch, knee bent. I moved my plate so that it rested on my thigh. "So what did they do? Obviously, the Dark Ages ended and society moved forward, so I'm assuming the good guys won."

He nodded. "They did, but at great sacrifice. At the time, the primary governance of good magic was overseen by a group of the most powerful witches in the world. Thirteen of them, to be exact."

I leaned over and reached for the bottle of wine, groaning when my back wouldn't bend in that direction far enough to reach it. "So that's not just magical lore? A coven actually has thirteen witches in it?"

He smiled and plucked the bottle off the table, then refilled our glasses. "Thirteen is more of a guideline. There is some magic in numbers, but the main reason there were thirteen in that coven is just because that's all that was left. At one point, they had nearly a hundred members. The dark forces had slaughtered the rest of them, one by one. That's when the coven did the only thing that had even a remote chance of turning the tide."

I was so entranced in the story that I hadn't even eaten my pizza. I took a big bite when he paused. "And what was that?"

He pointed toward my necklace. "They came together and sacrificed themselves, pouring all of their magic into the stone around your neck. All but one of them, that is. They chose one, the most powerful of all of them, to wield the stone and defeat the darkness."

That was a whole lot to process, so I ate the rest of my slice in silence. "So she defeated them by herself?"

He shook his head. "No, nobody could've done that. The forces had grown too great. She carried the power of her sisters, but even that wouldn't have been enough. Before she mounted her attack, she gathered an army of magical beings, though army is probably too big of a word. She chose the strongest and the most powerful from each clan. Shifters, fae, waterfolk, anybody that was left, and she asked them to fight with her. They did, of course, because they were being slaughtered as surely as witches were."

I touched the stone around my neck. "She was my ancestor, wasn't she? This woman who led an army of magical beings was my great, great, great, whatever grandmother?"

He nodded. "Now you're catching on."

"But then, what about my father's ring?"

He glanced at me, his expression approving. "Good catch. They used a sliver of the stone to make a ring for her most trusted advisor. Through it, he had access to a small amount of her power, and they could communicate from anywhere. Somewhere through the centuries, the advisor's line was lost, and the ring returned to your family."

I drew my brows together. "How do we not know how or when that happened? What was the bloodline? That has to be recorded somewhere, right?"

He shrugged. "I'm sure it was, but legend has it that at some point, the advisor betrayed his mistress, and she purged his line from history. We have no way to tell who it is, and believe me, people have tried to find out."

That explained the Dark Ages problem, but I wasn't sure what it had to do with my dad. "I understand why that much power was needed back then, but why did it carry forth after her? Why not just one-and-done?"

He popped the last bite of his pizza into his mouth, then washed it down with a drink of wine. "That's not the first or the last time the forces of darkness have made a power grab. It just happened to be the closest they ever came to succeeding. The Mistress of Balance stands between the forces of evil and the forces of good. There has to be both in the world, but there can't be too much of either. You're familiar with the Yin and Yang symbols right?"

I rolled my eyes. "I might be new to this whole magic thing, but I *have* lived on the planet for forty-nine years. I know about Yin and Yang."

"Then consider yourself the line that runs between them. We need darkness in the world too, as bad as we hate to admit it, so there needs to be a balance. And that's you."

I squeezed the bridge of my nose. "Holy geez. No pressure, then?"

He laughed and patted me on the knee as he stood to take our plates to the kitchen. "No pressure."

You'd have thought finding out I was the one person standing between the powers of good and evil would've been enough to scare the bejeezus out of me, but you'd have been wrong. Though I was dying to ask Ronan more questions, he'd already spent more than an hour telling me the story. The least I could do was let him watch a movie in peace.

Not that I was surprised, but I found myself having a great time with him. In fact, I hadn't enjoyed anybody's company other than CiCi's and Laurel's as much as I did his in a very long time. He had a sharp but corny sense of humor that I could relate to, and he wasn't one of those people who either talked so much that you couldn't watch the movie or got irritated when you made a comment. I was a little sad when the movie ended because it meant our night was over.

When the credits started to roll, he looked around. "The apartment really outdid itself. It's like a brand-new place, and if you'd have seen it when your dad lived here, you wouldn't even recognize it as the same place. You mind showing me around?"

"Sure," I said wincing when I stood. Now that I knew he was much older than I was, it was a little annoying that he didn't snap, crackle, and pop every time he moved too.

"What are the odds that now that I've claimed my magic, some of these aches and pains will go away? And maybe a few of the crow's feet and fine lines along with them?" I figured I'd keep it delicate rather than asking what I really wanted to know—would some of the effects of gravity be erased? I could certainly stand a nip here or a tuck there.

He chuckled. "I've already told you you're perfect just the way you are, but if you're that worried about it, I'd say there's probably at least a chance your magic has some sort of healing side effect. Historically, your line has longer-than-average lifespans."

"Great," I said, rolling my eyes. "I'd probably still look and feel thirty if I'd claimed my magic earlier." I led him down the hallway. "I'm assuming you've seen the back part of the house?"

He nodded. "The whole back area was one large bedroom with the master bath."

I gave him a quick tour and did my best to rush him back out of my bedroom. I wasn't fast enough, though.

He stopped exactly where I'd been afraid he would and turned to me with arched brows. "Mind explaining why there's a sock sticking out of your drywall?"

I made a point of looking at my feet and shrugged. "Not sure. Maybe it's just left over from when my dad was here."

His lips curved into an amused smile. "Yeah, because your dad was a real fan of pink-and-blue striped socks." He pointed a stern finger at me. "No more magic until you're in a safe space and I'm with you."

"What about Eddie and Erik?" It seemed to me that since they were wizards, they'd be qualified to work with me.

He sighed. "Your dad told you to come to me. He had his reasons, and though I trust the guys, I feel like it's important to respect your dad's wishes. I can't tell you what to do, of course, but I can request that you let me help you. I do have my own brand of magic and a few other tools in my box."

I couldn't help the slightly lascivious grin that spread across my face. "I just bet you do." I didn't particularly mean to say anything out loud, but when those blue eyes turned a smoky, smoldering gray, I wasn't sorry that I had.

In a flash, the air around us thickened with desire. I licked my lips, and his gaze landed on my mouth. The pit of my belly warmed, and I leaned toward him.

Gently, he cupped my face in his hands and leaned in, but at the last minute, he raised his lips and kissed me on my forehead. "I'm trying to respect that you're in an emotionally fragile state, but just looking at you drives me wild. This isn't over, but it's over for tonight."

He ran his thumb along my jawbone, then fluttered a kiss along my cheek. "Thanks for having me over. I'll see you tomorrow."

I showed him out, then climbed in bed and dreamed of a sexy, blue-eyed wolf shifter and ancient witches performing rituals under the moonlight.

Chapter Fifteen

Since I had nothing on my agenda for the day, I lazed around the house and hung out on the deck. I ate my breakfast out there, hoping to run into the stupid bird. Halfway through my bagel, my phone rang from inside, and I went in to grab it. By the time I came back, the bagel was gone, and Lapis sat in the tree, picking at it with his beak. I debated breaking the no-magic rule and sending just a tiny little bolt of lightning toward him but stopped myself at the last minute. The last thing I needed to do was set the tree on fire, and I *had* promised Ronan I wouldn't try any more magic until he had a chance to work with me.

I could, however, pluck a nice-sized rock out of one of the planters. I drew my arm back and winged it at him as hard as I could. I was happy to see that my time on the company softball team had paid off. I missed him, but it did knock the bagel off the limb and into the sand below.

I crossed my arms and smirked at him. "I might not have it, but now you won't either. At least not without swallowing a ton of sand."

He tilted his head and gave me the hairy eyeball with

his one good eye before he flew away. He squawked in his stupid parrot-y voice as he flew past me. "Hateful witch."

I snagged another rock out of the planter, and this time, even though he was a moving target, I landed a bullseye. I scrambled for an insult to fling along with it, but he was gone before my brain returned anything. At least today, I felt like I'd leveled the score.

I snagged my coffee from the table and slipped back inside, debating what to do next. The pink on my arms had turned to tan, so I decided to hit the beach for a bit.

It hit me when I picked up my foot to put on my bathing suit bottom that the movement came easily. Usually I had the grace and agility of a pregnant camel, but I got both legs in on the first try without falling over once. Miracle of miracles! When I straightened back up, I wasn't even a little stiff.

I rushed to the bathroom mirror and was disappointed to find the wrinkles still settled in their normal spots. I pushed the skin on my cheeks back a little, then did the same with my jaw. Before I'd left Rob, I'd been considering a micro facelift. Now that I was living at the beach and interacting with other people, most of whom were older than I was, I found I had no interest in that anymore. I shrugged. Even if my magic only took away the aches and pains, I'd be happy with that.

This time, I pulled three bottles of water from the fridge and stuffed them in my beach bag along with my sunscreen and book. I wasn't going to dehydrate like I had the last time. With my beach bag in one hand and my purse in the other, I headed downstairs.

"Hey, girl!" a feminine voice called.

I turned to find Janelle leaning against the bar. "What's up? Heading to the beach?"

I paused and forced a smile across my face. It's not that I wasn't glad to see her, but I already had the beach and a book on my brain, and I wasn't particularly looking for company. She was a guest, though, so I figured it was best not to pretend I hadn't heard her.

"Hey, yourself. I didn't expect to see you here." I walked around the bar and joined her, slinging my bag and my purse onto the stool between us.

She smiled as she slid onto the stool. "I hadn't planned to stop, but my client canceled, and I found myself with nothing to do. Did you sign up for the class tonight?"

I glanced at her, nonplussed. "No. I didn't realize I had to."

She nodded. "Yeah, she has a Facebook group, and you just go there and pay your fee." She pulled out her phone and tapped it a couple times, then turned it toward me. "This is her page."

I chatted with her for a few minutes while I signed up but then prepared to make my excuses. Before I could, though, the morning's coffee pressed so hard on my bladder that I knew I better go before I headed down to the water. "Would you mind watching my stuff while I run to the bathroom?"

She flapped a hand at me. "Of course. Go do your thing."

I had my Pokémon app up on my phone and was looking at it when my toe caught on the crack of an uneven board. I fell forward, my phone skidding across the floor, and braced for a face plant. Much to my absolute delight, my fall stopped when my nose was about a foot off the ground, and not one square inch of me other than my toes touched the floor. Now *that* was gonna come in handy!

I spent the rest of the day doing various forms of nothing, which was nice after the mad rush that had been my life for the last week. My night ended in moderate disappointment though when Janelle didn't show up for the class and didn't take my calls, either. Flaky people irritated me, and I'd think twice before I wasted my time making plans with her again.

Still, I had a new octopus painting that I was actually proud of, so it wasn't a total waste. It would be the first personal stamp I put on my new home, and that made me happy.

Chapter Sixteen

At five the next morning, I woke to the sound of somebody trying to pound my door down. I jumped out of bed, nearly killing myself when my feet tangled in the sheets. Oddly, I felt extreme agitation, but it didn't set off any inner alarms. I somehow knew it was Ronan.

"What the hell?" I snapped when I jerked the door open. I tended to be cranky when woken out of a dead sleep.

He pushed his way in, every muscle in his body tense. "You didn't even ask who it was before you opened the door."

I blinked, trying to get my brain awake enough to deal with him. "So, what? You just about broke my door down in the middle of the night just to make sure I don't open it for strangers?"

He waved a hand as he paced. "Of course not. Don't be ridiculous."

My temper flared as I scrubbed the sleep from my eyes.

I'd had enough of people talking down to me for a lifetime, and I crossed my arms over my chest. "Excuse me, but from where I'm standing, I'm not the one being ridiculous. If you can't be civil, you can haul your ass right back out the way you came."

He stopped pacing and pulled in a deep breath as he pinched the bridge of his nose. "You're right. I called my mother after our talk the other night to see if I could find out a little more about your family history. You seemed genuinely curious, so I thought I could give you some answers."

"Okay" I said, drawing the word out. "That was nice of you, but obviously whatever you found out wasn't fabulous."

I let that hang, giving him an opening to continue. While he gathered his thoughts, I went about making my latte. He waited for me to finish grinding the beans before he spoke, and I wasn't sure if that was out of courtesy or because he wasn't sure where to start with the story.

"No," he said. "It was the opposite of good. She didn't get back to me until this morning. It seems your father was dealing with something on his own, which wasn't like him at all."

"Did she find out what he was working on?" Anxiety began to build in my chest, and dread slid its cold finger down my spine. Between what Dad had written in his note and what Ronan had told me, it felt almost like premonition.

"Yes and no. It seems a wizard named Drake is trying to drum up power in Northern Ireland. From what we can gather, your father wasn't a hundred percent sure there was a threat, so he went to check it out himself before he alerted anybody else. That wasn't the greatest idea, but I can see why he didn't want to sound the alarm if there wasn't a threat."

I frothed my milk and poured it over into my mug, not bothering with trying to make a design like I normally did. "Not that you seem like you need caffeine, but would you like some coffee?"

His gaze shot to the espresso machine, and he nodded. "Caramel mocha latte, just like you're drinking, and I'll have a bagel while you're making them too. Veggie cream cheese, not honey."

I popped an eyebrow up. I can sort of understand how he knew what coffee I was drinking even though the beans weren't labeled and the syrups were in decorative squeeze bottles. After all, it was the same coffee I usually drank. There was no way he could have known I had veggie cream cheese. Even if he'd peeked in my fridge the night he'd been there, I'd just bought it the day before. For that matter, I hadn't even mentioned I was making a bagel.

"How did you know all that?"

He stopped pacing and turned to me with a questioning look. "How did I know all what?"

I added fresh grounds to the espresso basket and twisted the cup into the machine. "What kind of coffee I'm making and that I was making a bagel, and even the type of cream cheese I had. You didn't ask if I had veggie cream cheese. You told me you wanted it."

He went absolutely still and tilted his head. "I'm not sure, but I just knew. I mean, I suppose I could've just assumed you're making a bagel since that's what you always have for breakfast, but I have no idea how I knew the details."

I took the bagels out of the bread box, then pulled out

two and popped them into the toaster oven. "Admittedly, what I know about real magic could fit in a thimble with space left over, but between that happening to me with the pizza the other night and it just happening to you with breakfast, I think we should consider that we're somehow connected. What, exactly, was your relationship with my father? Could you do that with him?"

He leaned against the counter and crossed one arm over his body, resting his other elbow on it as he rubbed his jaw. Despite the situation, I couldn't help but notice how hot the extra stubble was on him. I reached a hand up to try to smooth the bedhead I had to be rocking.

He spoke, dragging my brain back to the situation at hand. "We were sort of partners for a lot of years. I knew him well enough that I could often anticipate his next move or guess what he was thinking, but it was never absolute knowledge like it just was with you. That wasn't even a conscious thing. It was just there as surely as if it were from my own experience."

Now I was the one getting anxious. I might have lived my life not knowing about magic, but I'd never been a believer in coincidence, and I knew in my soul that everything happened for a reason. When I combined that with the very real sense of foreboding in my gut, which I also always followed, the math added up. Something was coming, and Ronan and I would need each other.

"How much was your mother able to find out about this Drake person?"

He sighed and pressed his lips together. "She had to talk to several different people, but she managed to piece together that he's gathered a lot more power than he should have without drawing attention to himself. Worse, word's already traveled about your existence. Mom didn't have any details, but she did know that Arnie's secret daughter had stepped onto the board."

My hand started to shake as I frothed his milk. "What board? Up until a couple days ago, I didn't even know magic existed, let alone that there was a game going."

"That's exactly what my mother was most concerned about. It won't take long for anybody to dig through your history and figure out that you've been oblivious up 'til now. She's afraid Drake will up his timeline and try to make a move before you can do anything to stop him."

Helplessness threaded with fear washed over me. "So, what do we do? I'm a fast learner, but like you said, most people have a lifetime to develop their magic. It's an intrinsic part of who you are. That's not the case with me, and I'm not sure if it ever will be."

He took the tin of milk from my hand and laid his hand on my shoulder. All the extreme emotion I'd sensed when he'd arrived evaporated, replaced by a quiet determination. It was a little strange to me that I could sense his emotions so distinctly. I'd always been intuitive, but this went way beyond just reading people.

"Look at me," he said.

I did as he asked and found compassion and understanding in his eyes. "You were born for this despite the fact that your father did everything in his power to shield you from it. Without even trying or knowing it was possible, you summoned a hurricane out of thin air on one occasion and fire on another. Those are skills it takes most people years to master, if they ever do. We'll start your training immediately, but I believe it's more a matter of trusting yourself and the power of your ancestors more than anything else. And finding the volume," he added with a small smile.

I pulled in a deep breath as I gathered the cream cheese

and paper plates. Magic may have been a foreign concept to me, but organization and efficiency were not. My experience gained from years of being president of the PTA and strategizing to stay on top of business competitors kicked in.

"I'm gonna need all the information we can get on Drake, and we need to build a team and a network. I'll leave that part to you because it's completely outside of my wheelhouse. I wanna start my training today, and I think we need to build a core team here. I like them as people, but can Erik and Eddie be trusted? Something tells me we're gonna need all the help we can get."

He thought about that for a moment, and I both appreciated and worried a little that he didn't have an instant answer.

He chewed on his lip but eventually nodded his head. "They were never part of anything your father and I worked on, but I've known them since they moved here. And, honestly, at this point, I don't think we have a choice."

Frustration coursed through me. I hadn't been lying when I'd said I was a fast learner, but I'd learned early on how to use tricks and shortcuts to move things from my short-term memory to my long-term. Now, I felt like I needed to read every book in the Library of Congress, but I only had time for a children's bedtime story.

A smile spread across my face as a solution presented itself. I'd learned two of the most important parts of being a good leader were having a right-hand person and being able to delegate. As soon as it occurred to me, I knew it was the right move.

"What?" he asked when he glanced up at me from making his coffee.

"My father told me to trust you, and we obviously have

some sort of connection. I can't learn all this on my own in the time we have, but you already have a lot of the knowledge I need." I paused and took a deep breath. I knew what I was suggesting was taking our relationship to a new level. "I think you should wear the ring."

As soon as I said the words, a sense of rightness settled over me, and I held my breath while I waited for his response.

He whipped his gaze toward me and responded without taking so much as a heartbeat to think about it. "Absolutely not."

I drew my brows down, confused. "Why not? It's the obvious solution. There seems to be a natural flow of information between us that could come in handy for us both. Plus, you're the only person Dad mentioned by name that I can trust. There might come a time when we'll need an open channel of communication. Even without putting any effort into it, we're already doing it. My gut tells me the ring and necklace would enhance that."

He closed his eyes. "And are you sure that's a good thing? That's big magic, Jules, and I'm not sure it can be undone if either of us change our mind later."

That mental lightbulb flickered on in my brain, shedding light on the underlying issue. I had faith in *him* because, to be honest, I had no choice. I'd been tossed over a cliff with no parachute, and he was the only one I knew who had one. My gut told me to trust him, and it had never steered me wrong.

I, on the other hand, had very little to offer him. He barely knew me. At least in the beginning, the information exchange would be a one-way street, and I surely seemed like more of a liability than an asset to him. In essence, I was requesting unhindered access to his knowledge, and he had no way to know if he could trust me. It was a huge ask.

I laid my hand on his arm. "If everything you've told me is true, then we know two things for a fact. One, I'm a key player. Two, we don't have much time. I realize you're getting the shit end of the stick out of the partnership at least for now, but maybe fate or the universe or the goddess or ... whatever you wanna call it put us together and linked us for a reason."

He ground his teeth together. "I'm the alpha of a very large pack. I'm not used to playing second to anybody, and frankly, I'm not comfortable doing it now."

I drew my brows down and tilted my head. "Who's asking you to play second? From where I see it, you're holding all the cards."

"For now," he replied, his expression dark. I could feel the conflicting emotions rolling off of him, but I didn't tell him that.

Ronan raked a hand through his hair. "But what happens when you come into your magic fully? I'm nobody's lap dog, and by all accounts, you'll be the most powerful magical being in the world."

"Would being the instigator of that really be a bad thing?" I asked softly. "You'd be my most trusted advisor. Hell, you already are. By the very definition of that, what you say would weight my every decision."

He huffed out a breath and waved his hand. "This isn't a decision I'll make in the spur of the moment. I need time to think about it."

I shrugged. Though I would've preferred he felt the rightness of it and took me up on my offer right now, I understood where his head was at. "Fair enough. When can we start my training?"

He barked out a laugh entirely lacking in humor. "I don't think we have any choice but to start immediately. Today. Even if the guys can't make it, I know enough to get you started."

I nodded. That would have to be good enough for now.

Chapter Seventeen

"Try again," Ronan barked, arms crossed and brow furrowed in consternation. He reminded me of a drill sergeant, and I had to fight the urge to be perverse. He hadn't been lying when he'd told me he was an alpha used to giving orders. Since I was naturally that way too, it went against my grain, and I understood why he was hesitant to wear the ring.

"That *was* me trying," I snapped, swiping the sweat off my forehead with my wrist. We'd been at it for hours, and I felt like I'd run a triathlon. Every muscle in my body was shaking, and I was pretty sure my brain was half melted.

He scowled at me. "Then try harder."

Rather than argue, I turned my frustration to the glass bottle two dozen yards downrange from me. I held my palms out and willed it to levitate. I managed to get it a couple inches off the two-by-four it was sitting on before it blew up. I growled in frustration.

Ronan scowled. "You're using a sledgehammer to crack a nut. Magic is a manipulation of energy, so you can't use more than your target can handle."

He wasn't saying anything he hadn't preached at least twenty times already, but I pulled in a deep breath and reminded myself that time was limited. Rather than respond, I focused on the last bottle remaining on the board. What I'd done so far obviously wasn't working, so I put my hands on my hips and racked my brain for a different approach.

Bryan was as stubborn as I was, and with his struggle with math and science, I'd had to be patient and sometimes take a different approach to get him to understand an equation or theory. I decided that experience may work in my favor here too, so I took a minute and thought before I tried again. Instead of concentrating on the bottle like I had been, I turned my attention to the air around it and willed it to gather around the bottle and lift it up. To my immense relief, the bottle rose and hovered a foot or so in the air.

Once it stayed there without blowing up for a few seconds, Ronan grinned and nodded in approval. "Excellent. That's how it's done. What did you do differently?"

I willed the air to relax its hold on the bottle, and it settled back in its original spot. Once there, it teetered and fell over, but I was taking the win.

"I called on the air rather than trying to lift the bottle itself."

His grin widened. "Normally, I'd call that cheating, but in this case we're going to say you found an alternate tactical solution and went with it. It got the result you wanted, so that's all that matters."

I laughed. "Where were you when my oldest son was in ninth grade and could look at an algebra problem and instantly find the answer in his head? I butted heads with his teacher for half the semester because he insisted that Derek needed to show his work."

Ronan shook his head, but the corners of his eyes remained crinkled with humor. "Normally, that's how I'd teach you too, but right now, we're results-oriented. We can fine-tune you later."

I rolled my eyes as I downed half my bottle of water in one go. "Oh, you mean like when we're not rushing to save the world from an evil wizard? File that sentence under words I never thought I'd say."

He lifted a shoulder and chucked me on the chin. "Welcome to the big leagues, kid."

We hadn't been able to reach Erik and Eddie, and I had to wonder if my progress wouldn't have been a little faster working with somebody who could actually do what Ronan was trying to teach me. If wishes were horses, beggars would ride, though, so I was more than willing to take the help being willingly offered.

"Ready to combine some elements?" Ronan asked.

My stomach rumbled, and I shook my head. "I'm running on empty. If I don't get some food in me, I'm gonna fall over."

He glanced at the clock on his phone, looking a little surprised. "I didn't realize we've been at it for so long. It's one o'clock, so I guess I can allow a lunch break."

I arched a brow. "Allow? You've whipped this nag about as hard as you can. It's not a matter of permission unless you want me to keel over dead."

I'd meant it as a joke, but it was a little closer to the truth than I cared to admit. My legs were quivering so hard it was all I could do to stand, and my brain was fogging over.

When Ronan had offered to train me, I'd assumed we'd be going to some desolate stretch of beach. Instead, he'd brought me to a large warehouse that, at first glance, appeared deserted. I'd been shocked when what appeared to be a dilapidated building turned out to be a state-of-the-art magical training facility.

"I still can't believe this place exists," I said, stuffing my water bottle and towel into my duffel bag. "How do they keep it a secret from humans?"

He cast me a wry look, and it didn't take a genius to interpret it as *duh*. "What did you think of it when we pulled into the lot?"

I shrugged. "That it was an abandoned warehouse. But that doesn't preclude kids and homeless people from being curious or lookin' for a place to get out of the rain."

He shook his head as he gathered his own bag. "No, it doesn't, which is why there are a couple of different layers of security. First, there's a repulsion spell on the building. Anybody who tries to come in is compelled to turn around and go in the other direction. If that doesn't work, the inside is glamoured to fit the image of the external appearance. All a human would see when they walked in the place is a building in such disrepair that it's about to fall in."

He smiled as he hoisted both of our bags onto his shoulder. "In fact, Jason, one of the owners, is brilliant. As soon as the front door opens and a non-magical being is detected, beams appear to fall. So far, it's been an effective deterrent, and the place has been here since the sixties."

I lifted a shoulder as I followed him out of the room and into the main corridor. The place was set up sort of like a private gun range with multiple rooms set up for different types of training. "However they've done it, I'm glad it's here."

He looked at me sideways, his lips curving into a boyish grin. "Even if you did spend half the morning getting your ass kicked by twelve-year-olds?"

I swerved sideways and bumped him with my shoulder

as we walked. "Not funny. Those kids were mean, especially the little fox shifter who bit me. I should probably get a tetanus shot."

He laughed. "He wouldn't have bitten you if you hadn't tried to take the last pack of fun-sized M&Ms out of the rewards basket."

I scowled. "I was there first, fair and square."

He shook his head and chuckled. "We were in the kids training area. The treats aren't meant for adults."

"There was no sign that said that," I replied, lifting my chin. "I refuse to feel guilty. I'm old and need the extra energy."

He paused as we came to the main door and raked his gaze over me from head to toe. "You don't look old to me. In fact, I noticed a decided lack of creaking and groaning today while we were working. Anything you'd like to share?"

I shivered as the heat of his gaze sent goosebumps over my arms and tried to toss a mental bucket of water over the fire that burst to life in my belly. "Maybe. I noticed yesterday that most of my aches and pains have gone away, and my flexibility has improved more than any yoga class could have caused."

He waggled his brows and grinned. "Flexibility, huh? I wouldn't mind testing the limits of that."

Heat crept into my face as I tried to push aside the mental images of all the ways I could make that possible.

I was saved from answering when the sunlight and heat smacked me like a physical punch as soon as we walked out the door. If I hadn't already been drenched in sweat, that would've done it. My water bottle was poking out the top of my bag, so I plucked it out and finished it. This heat was going to take some getting used to, but I was starting to believe it was worth it.

Ronan took me to a burger joint that he swore was the best in town. One bite in, and I was a believer. We were just finishing up when his phone rang, and he pivoted it toward me so I could see who was calling.

Eddie's face smiled from the screen. Ronan explained why he'd called but kept it only to the fact that I was starting my training.

"Okay, great," he said, nodding. "We're heading back to the warehouse now, so we'll meet you there."

Once he disconnected the call, I questioned why he'd kept it vague.

He sighed and scrubbed a hand over his face. "As bad as I hate it, I'm not comfortable putting all of our trust in them, at least not yet. There may come a time when we need them, but that hasn't come yet."

Considering a guy named Drake was trying to cause some kind of Armageddon, that didn't make sense to me. "Wouldn't it be best if we had all hands on deck?"

He wobbled his head back and forth. "Maybe, but in my experience, single practitioners with only an average amount of magic can be more of a hindrance than an asset. The biggest advantage members of packs and covens have is that they're used to operating both independently and as just one piece of a larger puzzle. There's power in numbers, and when you have to combine forces like we probably will, you need people used to working as part of a larger unit. Another advantage is that even though I have over five hundred adults in my pack, I know every single one of them's strengths and weaknesses and can use that when I strategize."

That was a staggering number to me. "How do you manage so many people?"

He lifted a shoulder. "Normally, it's not an issue. Just

like humans, we go about our everyday lives unless we have to come together as a pack. That rarely happens, but we still train regularly. I've broken them down into ten sub-packs of fifty or so people based on skill set and personality. Mostly, that hasn't required much work on my part. It's kind of been handed down from one generation of clans to the next."

That gave me a lot to think about on the way back, and my respect for him shot up several notches.

The guys were waiting for us at the warehouse when we got back, and I was feeling much better than I had when we'd left. The food and rest had done me good, and I was ready to get back to it. The sense of urgency that had started as a niggle of worry in my gut that morning had built steadily throughout the day.

Even without the warning from Ronan's mother, I had a feeling I would've known something was coming. At least now I knew and could be prepared. With that in mind, I doubled down on my effort, determined to fulfill my role in whatever was to come.

Chapter Eighteen

Over the next few days, my life boiled down to training, eating, and sleeping. Strangely, Ronan's mood grew steadily worse, and when I asked him about it, he waved me off with some variation of, "It's nothing. I just have a lot on my mind, and we need to focus on your training."

At the end of the fourth day, he was absolutely unbearable. "I don't even know why we're trying. Instead of putting our faith in a human that's lived most of her life not even knowing magic exists, I should be gathering the clans and covens and developing a strategy."

I was bent over with my hands on my knees, trying to catch my breath after starting a magical fire and then extinguishing it with a combination of sand and water. Considering I'd gone from being unable to lift a single bottle off the table without busting it to successfully combining three different elements in just a matter of days, it was safe to say I didn't think he was being fair.

"That's it!" I snapped, snatching my water bottle off the bench. "I've been bustin' my ass twelve hours a day trying to get a handle on my magic, then going home and spending two hours learning the new spells the book keeps throwing at me. And if that's not enough, I spend another two hours reading all the magical history books your mother sent. I don't know what else I can give you."

At mention of his mother, his back stiffened. "Yeah, you and Mom have become fast friends, haven't you?"

I glared at him, trying to figure out why he'd said that as if I'd been flirting with the devil. "Your mom's been a huge help to the both of us. She's doing her best to help me from afar, and she's gathering the clans and covens in Europe. A little gratitude on your end might be nice."

Not that he hadn't been doing the same thing in the States at the same time he was training me, but I couldn't understand why he was acting like such an ogre to us when he was fine and dandy to everyone else. To top it off, his emotions toward me flip-flopped between intense resentment and fervid attraction, causing a maelstrom that made it almost impossible for me to concentrate sometimes. I wanted nothing more than to be able to block that out, but as mercurial as he was being, admitting I could feel his emotions didn't seem like a fabulous idea. Instead, I did my best to teach myself.

His shoulders sagged at the mention of his mom. "She thinks I should take the ring."

Rather than throwing up my hands in irritation, I took a deep breath. After what we'd been through over the last week, I was having problems understanding why he was so hesitant. My lack of understanding didn't change the issue though.

I took a seat on the bench and wiped the sweat from my face and the back of my neck with a towel. "I don't know what to say to that. I agree because somehow, I know in my gut it's the right thing to do."

He looked away, flexing his jaw. "And that's the problem. Every fiber of my being is telling me to resist."

I searched his gaze. "Are you sure about that? Or is it just that you're fighting your natural instinct to lead independently? We've been training nonstop, and you have to be as exhausted as I am. Why don't you take the rest of the afternoon and evening to do something besides focus on Drake and this entire mess?"

He stared at me for a moment, then snatched his duffel bag off the bench and stormed toward the door. "Thanks. I think I will."

After he left, I continued practicing. I'd gotten to the point that I knew my magic well enough to test its limits. Every night, the grimoire gave me new spells to build upon what I'd learned that day. Between it and the drills Ronan, Erik, and Eddie put me through, my skills seemed to double every day. I spent the next couple of hours breaking clay pots, glass bottles, and boards down into their natural elements. After I had gone through several of each with little effort, I decided to try to reverse the process and put them back into their original forms. I didn't have as much luck doing that, but I did have some success. When I finally managed to get the pile of sand back into the shape of a glass bottle, I called it a day.

I'd half expected Ronan to be at the bar when I got home, but he wasn't. I squelched the disappointment in my chest and slid onto a stool.

Lavonne, one of my afternoon bartenders, smiled and slid a glass of my favorite IPA in front of me. "Rough day?" she asked.

I huffed out a tired breath and took a big swig of the beer. "You have no idea. How have things been here?"

Several people in swimsuits sat around the bar, eating, chatting, and enjoying the weather. Bob Marley's "Three Little Birds" drifted from the jukebox, and I sat back, sipping my beer and absorbing the relaxed vibe.

I'd almost finished my first one when a sharp burst of anger mixed with loathing stabbed my mental barrier. I swiveled my head, looking for Ronan. If he was still on the warpath, I was in just the frame of mind to adjust his attitude. When I didn't see hide nor hair of him, I bit my lip, confused. If it wasn't him, then who was it?

"Hey, girl!" a familiar feminine voice said from behind me. "I owe you a huge apology for not showing up the other night."

I pivoted on my stool, squirming a little bit when the animosity went up a notch. I had no sense of where it was coming from, and annoyance at myself for not having control over that washed over me. Doing my best to pull the fragile mental barrier that I'd worked hard to build down around me, I pasted on a smile for Janelle.

"Yeah, I tried to call you, but you didn't answer. In fact, it worried me a little."

That wasn't strictly true, but it was the right thing to say.

She slid onto the stool behind me, hooking her purse beside mine under the bar. "I'm really sorry. I lost my phone that day right after an important client called and wanted to view a piece of property."

Since a missed dinner date with somebody I hardly knew wasn't even a blip on my radar at that moment, I didn't waste too much emotional energy being mad at her. "It's fine. I'm sure we can get together another time."

The anger stabbed harder at my barrier, breaking through for a second before I could push it back out. I looked around the bar, trying to find the source, but everybody seemed to be laughing and having a good time.

"No," she said, smiling as Lavonne set her beer in front of her. "I swear, I'm never flaky like that. I really am sorry and would like to make it up to you."

Deciding I probably had enough enemies in the world at the moment, I decided to let bygones be bygones and spent the next hour and a half chatting with her about her business and life in general.

After about my fourth yawn, she patted my arm. "You poor thing. You look exhausted, and here I sit just jabbering away. I need to go home anyway, so how about I check the schedule for the next wine-and-painting event and let you know?"

I nodded and smiled because my heart was craving something human and normal. "That sounds great. Just let me know."

We said our goodbyes, and I made my way home. Even though I was exhausted, I figured it would be best to check the book for my newest lessons. Sure enough, there were three new spells, and I smiled. One was an elemental spell to call water from the air, but the other two were just what the doctor ordered for my most pressing needs. One was for blocking emotional energy, and the other was for detecting magic. I had no idea *how* the book always knew what I needed, but I was grateful.

I spent the next half hour memorizing them and trying to use them, but without a source of emotions, there wasn't much I could do on the practical side of things.

Ten minutes later, that problem solved itself when I felt Ronan coming up my stairs. Unlike the anger I'd felt in the bar earlier, his energy felt familiar. I huffed, annoyed that I hadn't picked up on that at the time. Whoever had been so pissy in the bar, it hadn't been Ronan.

I opened the door just as he was holding his hand up to knock, and he scowled. "I hate it when you do that."

I cocked a brow but didn't stand back to let him in. I wasn't ready to go another round with him, so if he was coming in with attitude, he could turn around and walk it right back to the parking lot. "Do what? Open the door to let you in?"

His scowl deepened. "You know that's not what I'm talking about. Are you going to let me in?"

I lifted a shoulder and stood my ground. "That depends. Are you here to be an asshole, or are you going to be civil?"

With a low growl, he closed the two steps between us and slid his fingers to the nape of my neck, then dropped his head and covered my lips with his. With my shields down, all that pent up desire and frustration slammed into me, full force. I leaned into him, winding one arm up around his neck and grasping the front of his shirt with the other. I'd wanted to do this for so long, and was glad that it was every bit as fabulous as I'd imagined.

He pushed me backwards and kicked the door shut, never taking his mouth off mine. Heat curled in my belly and spread outward as he deepened the kiss and slid his tongue into my mouth, joining it with mine. He groaned deep in the back of his throat and pulled me closer to him, winding his fingers through my hair. Every inch of my body pressed tightly against his, leaving no doubt as to his desire.

For a split second, logic pushed its way into the fog of lust clouding my brain, but I pushed it away. This wasn't me acting like some teenager ruled by lust. I'd wanted this man since the first moment I'd laid eyes on him, and I was sick of living my life based on arbitrary rules imposed on me by a pious society. I opened my senses and let the tempest of his emotions join with mine.

He trailed his mouth down the side of my neck, nipping the tender flesh under my ear, then bent and scooped me into his arms.

"You're mine," he growled against my ear, nuzzling it, and my heart raced. Moving his lips back to mine, he carried me to the bedroom and kicked the door shut behind us.

Chapter Nineteen

Two hours later, I curled into Ronan's side with my head on his shoulder and yawned. My entire body felt boneless, and for the first time in a long time, I was completely relaxed.

"That was nice," I said, drawing little circles on the mat of hair on his chest.

He chuckled, and I could feel the rumble of it under my cheek. "Nice wasn't exactly what I was going for, so maybe we should try again."

I grinned, then tilted my head up and kissed him on his jaw. "Are you fishing? Fine, then. It was great. Fabulous. Amazing. The best I've ever had."

He gave me a little squeeze. "That's more like it. I put in a lot of effort and appreciate the recognition."

At that, I laughed. "I'm pretty sure I gave you recognition at least a couple times. Would you like applause?"

He bent his head and nipped my lip. "No, but I do have a T-shirt that says Ronan is a Sex God if you wouldn't mind wearing it."

I rolled my eyes and poked him in the ribs. "Sure. Just let me know when your parents are coming, and I'll add it to my wardrobe."

"See," he said trailing his fingertips down my arm, "that's how I can tell you've never been around shifters. We pride ourselves on our virility. There's no shame in my game."

I couldn't argue with that, so I just snuggled closer, enjoying the peace and comfort.

"About my mother, though." He paused and pulled in a deep breath then released it. "I did as you suggested and took the afternoon to figure out what's really in my heart. Once I set aside my pride and my ego—which wasn't an easy thing for me to do—I realized you're right. I feel the calling to wear the ring too."

I pushed up on my elbow so I could see his face, then sighed. "Before you make your final decision, I have something I need to tell you."

He drew his brow down a little, the slightest hint of worry flashing through his eyes.

I bit my lip, wary of breaking the fragile new threads of our bond but knowing I had to confess so that he could go in with his eyes wide open. "I can feel your emotions."

He thought about that for a second, then shrugged. "I kinda figured that, because I can feel yours too. In fact, that's been part of the reason I've been so edgy the last few days. I know you're giving this your all, but things aren't coming together as quickly as I'd hoped. I feel like I'm letting you down."

I shook my head. "For a man so intelligent, you can be really dense. I've spent half my life organizing people and roping them into doing things they don't want to do. It was all I could do sometimes to convince people to bring cupcakes to the class party when it was their turn. I can't even imagine the response I would've gotten had I asked them to risk their lives. I knew going into this that we had an uphill battle, but we can only do what we can do. For what it's worth, I have faith in us."

He pulled me closer to him and kissed me on the forehead. "That might be your biggest strength. Even with everything you've been through, you can still see the light at the end of the tunnel."

I huffed against his shoulder. "Oh, I've always seen it, but I'll let you in on a little secret. Half the time, I'm convinced it's a train."

He shifted his weight so he was looking down on me, his face close to mine. "If you need me to slay a train, all you have to do is ask."

It was a little corny, but the kiss that followed it was full of such promise that I had no doubt it was true.

* * *

I slept like the dead, and woke up right as daylight began to filter through my curtains. Ronan snored softly beside me, and I took the time to examine him more closely. He was every bit as beautiful asleep as he was awake—maybe more. The anxious lines on his forehead and at the corners of his eye that I'd gotten used to were absent, and he looked serene.

I curled against him and tried to go back to sleep, but my brain was already awake. I slipped out of the bed and tiptoed from the room, unwilling to wake him. After pulling the door shut behind me, I stretched and winced a little. Muscles I hadn't used in a long time had gotten quite a workout, but for once, I was happy to be sore. If that was the price of one of the most magnificent nights of my life, I had no complaints.

I'd just finished making my coffee when he padded into the kitchen, still in his boxers.

"Morning, beautiful," he said wrapping his arms around me from behind and nuzzling my neck.

I leaned back into him and smiled. "Had I known all it took was a night of mind blowing sex to put you in a good mood, I'd have led with that."

He nipped my neck, then swatted me on the butt. "Smart-ass. Are you gonna make me a cup of that too?"

"If you're nice."

He waggled his brows at me. "I believe you told me last night that I was nice."

I handed him the cup of coffee I'd just finished and started a second cup. "Not to be a buzz kill, but are you sure about the ring?"

He blew across the top of the cup, then took a sip and nodded. "More now than ever, though I admit to having a selfish motive on top of a true desire to succeed for the sake of everybody. I wanna be able to make sure you're safe, and if the ring will help us do that, then count me in. Besides, I was being stupid and arrogant. You were right to view this as a partnership, and I was wrong to see it as some sort of hierarchy."

While my coffee brewed, I reached for my purse. "No time like the present, then, right?"

I dug through to find the zippered pouch, and a little burst of panic shot through me when it was open. At first, I thought maybe it had just dropped into the bottom of my purse, but when I moved things around, I couldn't find it.

Frantic, I pulled everything out one by one onto the counter. I got to the bottom and still couldn't find the ring, I felt as if all of the air had been sucked from the room.

"Jules! What is it?" Ronan covered the distance between us in two strides and put his arm on my shoulder.

"The ring," I said desperately digging through the mess of lipsticks, hair ties, wrappers, and receipts strung across my counter. I turned my purse upside down and shook it. "It's gone, Ronan! The fucking ring is gone!" I put my palm to my forehead, pacing and fighting the panic pressing in on me.

He strode toward the pile on the counter and dug through it himself. "Gone? What do you mean it's gone? You had it in your purse?"

I nodded and tried to swallow the total freak-out threatening to consume me. "Yeah. That's where I put it when I picked it up out of the safety deposit box. I know it sounds stupid, but I just didn't think to put it in the safe."

He took me by the shoulders, then tilted my chin so he could look in my eyes. "We'll find it."

"What if–"

He pulled me into his arms and stroked my hair. "Don't even think it. We'll find it."

He pushed his cup of coffee into my hand and guided me to the deck. "Sit right here. I'll make us some bagels and be right back."

I did my best to clear my mind so I could think logically. Lapis landed on the railing and squawked.

I glared at him. "Today's not the day, bird. You do not want to come up here and start shit, or so help me, I'll fry what few feathers you have left right off of you."

Apparently, he did have some sense of self-preservation because he just sat there quietly.

A few minutes later, Ronan joined me, sliding a bagel to me and taking a seat. Much to my surprise, he tossed a bagel at Lapis too, who caught it in midair.

I scowled at him. "Why'd you do that?"

He sighed and turned to the bird. "Okay, Lapis. Up 'til now, I've been content not to out you, but we need your help."

Confused, I glanced from Ronan to the parrot. "I don't follow."

As I said it, Lapis's form shimmered, and all of the color faded from him. His wings elongated as his feathers fell out, revealing a gray-brown skin underneath. He quadrupled in size, and his beaked head crunched and shifted until it was more bat-like than bird-like. When he spread his wings, they spanned at least twelve feet.

Though I had a hard time believing my eyes, I'd seen enough gargoyles on the buildings in Atlanta to know what I was looking at. As much as I thought I should be surprised, I really wasn't. I don't know whether that was because I was already in shock or because I'd just accepted that magic existed and recognized that this was just another new thing to absorb.

I scowled. "Are you tellin' me a gargoyle's been stealing my breakfast for the last week?"

Ronan covered his mouth, and I could tell he was doing his best not to laugh.

I turned to Lapis, scowling. "I almost broke my freakin' hand that first day when I punched you."

He lifted his shoulder, and when he spoke, his voice was gravelly. "That's what you get for attacking a poor defenseless bird."

"Defenseless?" My voice rose a couple octaves. "You took a chunk out of my thumb!"

He turned to Ronan, his expression bored. "I assume you have a better reason than giving her somebody to yell at for making me reveal myself?"

I snapped my jaw shut because he was right.

Ronan nodded. "We think the ring's been stolen."

Lapis hissed. "I thought I felt it last night, but I figured it was you."

"You mean all that anger? Down in the bar?" I struggled to remember all the faces, but I hadn't paid that much attention to any of them because they all appeared happy.

"Yes. It was so powerful that I felt it all the way up here."

I took a second to absorb what he was saying. "Wait, why did you think it was the ring? I thought I was the only one with a connection to it. Or rather, whoever's wearing the necklace."

He shifted his weight toward me a little bit. "I have a connection because I placed myself into service of the original mistress just as I now serve you."

"You don't—"

Before I could protest, Ronan laid his hand on my arm and shook his head. Though he didn't offer an explanation, I had a feeling it was a conversation for another time when we had privacy. I don't know how I knew that, but I did.

Following his lead, I put a pin in it and returned to the subject at hand. "Did you see who it was?"

Lapis didn't even try to hide his scathing expression. "No. When I saw you there, I assumed you were dealing with it. I should've known better." He pivoted so that he was staring at Ronan. "You're as much at fault as she is. Maybe more, because you know. Had you taken the ring when she offered it, things would be as they should be, and we wouldn't be in this mess."

Champagne Witches

I took a sip of my coffee but pushed the bagel aside. My appetite had evaporated when I'd found the ring missing. "Who'd want to steal it? What could possibly be gained?" Even before the questions left my lips, I knew the answer.

Anybody who had the ring had access to my thoughts.

Chapter Twenty

"When was the last time you saw the ring?" Ronan asked.

I racked my brain then shrugged helplessly. "When I put it in my purse. That was the day after I got here."

He squeezed the bridge of his nose, but before he could say anything, Lapis cut in, his tone flat. "Yeah, it's gone, then. The last time it went missing, we didn't find it for two hundred years."

His gravelly voice perfectly matched his appearance, and his accent reminded me of a New York gangster.

I glared at him, but directed my question at Ronan. "Why do we need him again?"

Ronan ran his tongue over his teeth. "Because he can sense the ring just like he can sense your necklace. You can too, or at least you'll be able to once you have full control of your powers. Are you sure the emotions you were feeling last night were attached to the ring?"

"It doesn't matter if she is or not because I am," Lapis

replied. "I know it as surely as I know the sun will rise in the morning."

I tapped my fingers on the table, thinking. "What's your range?"

The gargoyle tilted his head, sending bits of sand to the railing that spilled over onto the deck. "I don't follow. What do you mean?"

"She means," Ronan said, "how far away can you sense it?"

Lapis huffed a breath out through his nose. "Not far enough. Remember I just told you we lost it for two hundred years? You think it would've been gone that long if I could feel it anywhere?"

I glowered at him. "You don't have to be an ass, you know. We have enough going on here, and we genuinely need your help."

He stared at me, his expression bland. "It hasn't even been fifteen minutes since you threatened to fry all the feathers off of me. Pardon me if I'm not jumping for joy at the prospect of helping you."

Since he'd just declared he was in my service, I was so confused. If Ronan thought we needed him, though, I'd do my best to mend fences. I pulled in a deep breath through my nose and blew it out through my mouth. "I'm sorry, okay?"

"I don't believe you."

Well, the bird might've been stubborn, mean, and rude, but he wasn't stupid. It occurred to me that if he truly had sworn servitude to my line, I could probably compel him to be nice. Though the thought of that amused me, we didn't have time for games.

I tore off a chunk of my bagel and popped it into my

mouth, deciding to take another tack. "I know we have security cameras, but how much do they cover?"

"The entire bar and patio area, inside and out," Ronan replied. "I say we start there."

Lapis shifted his weight on the railing, and when it creaked, I wondered just how much a gargoyle made of stone weighed. For that matter, was he even actually made of stone? Did he actually turn into a parrot, or was that just a glamour? I shook off the disjointed questions.

He gave me the hairy eyeball for a second, and I wondered if he was able to read my thoughts. "The smart thing would be to figure out who had access to her purse."

I sighed, trying to think back. "It's been a week. I've been here, to the grocery store, and to the warehouse. That's it. I can guarantee you nobody got it at the grocery store or at the warehouse. My purse was never out of my sight at either of those places."

Ronan nodded. "Then that's good. We have a place to start."

I picked at my fingernail, thinking. "Do you think my house would let anybody in?"

Ronan sat for a second, thoughtful. "That's a good question, but one I don't have the answer to. Why? Was your purse in the house a lot while you weren't there?"

I lifted my shoulder. "Not that I can remember, but it's possible. Also there are other times like when I'm showering or sleeping when people could come in and take it."

The thought of somebody being in my house while I was there and helpless made me shudder. Based on the way Ronan narrowed his eyes and growled low in his throat, I assumed he wasn't any happier about it than I was. Despite the gravity of the situation, I smiled a little. It hadn't been too many hours ago that he was growling in pleasure rather than frustration or anger. A little shiver ran over my body at the memories, and when he looked at me, his eyes were that smoky blue-green, and I knew he was picking up on my emotions or my thoughts.

I finished off my coffee. "Let's go look at the security footage. We should be able to narrow it down to the times I was there, and I have a pretty good idea of when that was."

We stood and collected our plates.

"You gonna eat the rest of that bagel?" Lapis was practically drooling looking at my plate. Resisting the urge to be petty and take it inside with me, I tossed out a little bit of goodwill and handed it to him. I figured there might come a time in the near future when I would need his help. If all it cost me was a bagel, then I could swallow my pride.

Two hours later, we finally came upon something that threw up a red flag. It was the day I'd run into Janelle at the bar and asked her to watch my bags while I went to the bathroom. Both my bags and her purse were on that same stool, and all were out of sight of the camera, and at one point, she went through one of them.

I sucked in a breath. "That was the day she blew me off for that paint thing later in the evening, and she was here last night when I felt that burst of emotion too. And my purse was hanging on the same hook as hers. I went to the restroom at least once."

We flipped to that footage, and it was the same thing. Since the purses were under the bar, there was no way to tell whether she was getting something from hers or mine, though she didn't appear to put anything in or take anything out.

Ronan's muscles bunched in his back right before a wall of frustration slammed into my mental barriers, and he stood up so quickly that he almost knocked the office chair over.

I put a hand on his arm. Years of dealing with fighting kids had taught me not to jump the gun without absolute proof. "This is suspicious, but it doesn't prove anything. We watched both of them three times, and there's no way to tell whether she was getting into her bag or mine. Also, she's a regular here. It's not like she was out of place."

He paced in front of the desk. "Who then? She's the only viable suspect we have."

I placed my hands on the desk and leaned over it so that I was closer to him. "Yeah, but that's all she is—a suspect. I say we invite her up to my place for a glass of wine so Lapis can be there. Then we can monitor her behavior and hopefully sense if she has the ring."

He rubbed his jaw. "There are a lot of holes in that idea. Namely, it's not like she's going to wear it right in front of you."

"No, but maybe if we ask the questions right, I can tell if she's lying or maybe pick up some other emotion."

He arched a brow at me. "Have you ever been able to do that with anybody other than me?"

I shrugged. "No, but I've never tried, either. I need to go upstairs and check the book. I'm not sure how it happens, but it somehow seems to know what spells I need, and they just appear."

He stopped, then spun on his heel so that he was facing me. "Well, shit. Why didn't you say that to begin with? It could be that it's already given you a summoning spell, and all we had to do is use it."

Somehow I knew it wasn't going to be that easy, namely because things never are, but I figured I wouldn't dash his hopes until I found out for sure. After all, he knew a whole lot more about this world than I did.

Chapter Twenty-One

I called Janelle and left a message for her to call me. Since neither of us knew where she lived, I wasn't sure what else we could do. To fill the time, we decided to go upstairs and check out the book.

I brought it to the kitchen and laid it on the counter, then flipped through the pages to the last two spells I'd looked at. Ronan glanced at me, his expression blank. "A spell to detect magic?"

I shrugged and took a drink of my wine. "I suppose that would be a first step. It makes sense that we'd be wasting our time if she's not even magical."

He rubbed the nape of his neck. "Maybe, I guess. Is there anything else?"

I flipped the page, and sure enough, a new one had appeared. I pulled my phone out to translate the Latin to English. It annoyed me that the book did that sometimes. If it knew what spells I needed, then surely it knew I was illiterate in every language except English. As if it read my mind, words appeared in English at the top of the page. Spell to compel somebody to tell the truth.

Just because all of my reading had taught me that you don't use spells you don't understand, I still Googled the words, then scoffed. Veritatem dicere. Literally, *tell the truth*.

I grinned. "Now we're getting somewhere."

Ronan pressed his lips together and put his hand on my arm. "Jules, I don't know if that's a good idea. There are lots and lots of laws about compelling anybody to do anything, and they exist for a reason. Compelling other beings to do your will against theirs is the beginning of the slide into corruption of power. As the Mistress of Balance, you're going to be held to a higher standard."

"Yeah, but if we don't find that ring, we're gonna have a whole lot more to worry about than ethics 101."

I knew as I said the words that I was standing at the top of the slide. That's exactly what somebody with an utter disregard for anything but power would say to justify their actions. Nonetheless, I was right, and he knew it.

I thought for a second. So far, the book had only given me what I needed. "Has a mistress ever gone bad?"

He pressed his lips together and pushed them to the side for a moment. "That's an excellent question. I don't think so, but I don't know for sure."

My sliding door, which we'd left cracked earlier just a bit to let in the morning breeze, whooshed open. Lapis strode through, his motions jerky and disjointed as if he hadn't walked in that form in a very long time. Of course, if he was stone, that might cause some mobility issues as well.

"I can answer that question beyond a shadow of a doubt," he rasped. "No. A mistress has never been corrupted by her own power. The magic she wears around her neck is pure, and should she ever sully that, she'd lose her right to it."

I cringed when he stepped on my Roomba. I'd paid big bucks for that as a treat to myself, and now it was in a million pieces.

He approached the counter and peered over at the book. "What spells did it give you?"

"How to detect magic, and one to compel somebody to tell the truth," I replied.

He stared at the page for a few seconds, and I was surprised when I could sense great deliberation rolling off of him. I suppose I shouldn't have been, considering he'd admitted he was in service to me, whatever that meant, but I still felt a little like I was peeking into his undies drawer, and trust me—that wasn't a pleasant feeling.

He glanced up at me, moderate disgust rolling across his features. "Get over it. This is a two-way street, and I don't like sharing head space anymore than you do. It is what it is, but you can block it out just like I can. As far as the spell goes, the book wouldn't have given it to you if it didn't think it was the right thing for you to do. I say use it."

Ronan pressed his lips together, and though he didn't say anything for a long moment, his disapproval was plain. "I'll go along with it, but I don't like it."

Once the decision had been made, it was just a matter of waiting for Janelle to return our call. That feeling of urgency had only grown in my belly, so sitting still and waiting her out was out of the question.

"I need to go train," I replied. "Eddie and Erik had something to do this morning, but I can practice some of the stuff on my own, or you can teach me."

"I have a better idea," Lapis said. "Train with me. If it comes to hand-to-hand combat, I'll be one of your best tools."

For the life of me, I couldn't figure out that logic. I

mean, I understood how having a massive stone creature with sharp teeth and claws that could rip an enemy to pieces would come in handy, but I wasn't entirely sure how we could coordinate that. I was also struggling a little to realize this was my new reality. "How does that work, exactly?"

He huffed out a breath, then leaned his elbow on my counter, causing a crack in the beautiful marble. Hopefully, the house could fix it. "Your father was a good man, but he was an idiot for leaving you in the dark. I'm displeased that I have to clean up his mess by dealing with a witch who, by all rights, should have trained for this from birth. It's simple. I carry you on my back, and we can fight midair."

He pointed over his shoulder and gave me a look that clearly expressed he thought I was a drooling idiot. "Wings, see? I can fly. I'm fast, so I can also get you out of harm's way so you can fight another day if that's what needs to be done. I'm stone, so weapons can't penetrate me. I have teeth and talons sharp enough to shred even the thickest armor. Which of those traits don't sound like a good thing to you?"

Ronan shook his head so adamantly that he reminded me of a bobblehead doll. "Oh no. Not just no, but *hell* no. I won't have it. She can ride with me."

Though I hadn't seen him shift yet, just the thought of running my hands through his fur thrilled me somewhere in the back of my mind, but my temper spiked at the overbearing tone. I was done with men ruling my life.

In the heat of the moment, I dropped my guard, and his emotions merged with mine. I spun on him and jabbed at him with my finger. "You don't get to say what I do or don't get to do."

His eyes narrowed as his gaze drilled into mine. "You

don't even know what you're letting yourself in for. Flying's dangerous, and it takes years of training to master."

I stood my ground, squaring my shoulders and pulling myself up to my full height even though I was still almost a foot shorter than he was. I was willing to negotiate anything but my autonomy. This was a hill I'd die on, and it was better to establish that rule here and now.

Tension crackled between us, and my heart skipped a beat when his eyes fell to my lips. The anger burning in my chest shifted to desire as memories from the night before flooded through my brain.

Lapis cleared his throat, breaking the spell, then closed his eyes as if praying for patience. "You two need to get over this whole mercurial sexual-tension thing. If I have to go into battle with the two of you, I don't want that freaky shit runnin' through my head."

Despite myself, I laughed, and the remaining bubble of tension broke.

He met my eyes, and for the first time since I'd met him, his expression was earnest. "Please, Mistress. I've pledged myself to your line. It's my duty to keep you safe. If the wolf wants to share in that, I have no problem with it, but only a fool ignores one of the most powerful tools at her disposal."

I glanced at Ronan, knowing he wasn't going to be pleased with my decision, but Lapis was right. "Where can we practice where people won't see us? It's not exactly like somebody wouldn't notice a chunky redhead riding a gargoyle over the beach."

Ronan scowled at me. "You're not chunky. You're beautiful."

Lapis rolled his eyes. "Normally, you'd glamour us to be invisible, but since you don't know how to do that yet, I know a place a little bit inland where we can fly without being seen." He arched a stone brow at me and, for the first time ever, grinned. "That is, unless you don't mind flying over water."

That was one of the most horrifying ideas I'd ever heard. Images of me falling twenty stories straight into the gaping maw of a thirty-foot Great White were quite literally my two biggest nightmares merged into one. "Hard pass."

Rather than ride with us, Lapis transformed back into a parrot and agreed to meet us there.

Ronan was quiet on the ride. "If you don't want to do this, you don't have to."

I'd been doing my best to respect his privacy, so I had my shields up. It didn't take a genius to figure out what his problem was though. It was one of two things: he was either worried I'd fall or jealous. The last option was so ridiculous that I refused to even acknowledge it. "Are you afraid Lapis will let me fall?"

"I don't like it when your safety is in somebody else's control." He kept his eyes straight ahead, flexing his jaw. So it was the jealousy thing, then.

I was torn between being flattered, which was ridiculous, and wanting to whack him. Instead, I scowled. "I'll have you know that I almost face planted at the bar the other day but instinctively, my magic stopped me. I'm pretty sure if it kicked in when I was falling three feet, I'll have plenty of time to save myself from twenty stories up. Also, this isn't Lapis's first rodeo. He may not be my biggest fan personally, but he made it pretty clear he takes his duties seriously."

Since I had no desire to even engage on the whole jealousy thing, I changed the subject. "I started to deny that he was in service to me, and you stopped me. Why? For that matter, do you know how that all came about?"

He nodded. "I'm a little surprised you haven't come across that story in your history books. Back during the original battle before the Coven of Magic merged, one clan of gargoyles defected to the dark side. At the time, that would have been disastrous. Morgana, your ancestor, came up with a brilliant solution. Gargoyles won't fight members of their own clan, so she kidnapped the chieftain—Lapis. Nobody really knows what went on behind closed doors, but she locked herself in a room with him for five days. When they came out, he'd pledged his service to her and her line, and they'd sealed it with a spell."

I bit the inside of my lip, thinking about that. "So what was the catch? Surely, he wouldn't have just made an open-ended deal. There has to be a way to get out of it."

He glanced at me sideways, one side of his mouth curved into a half-smile. "That ancestor of yours was as clever as she was powerful. The details of the deal weren't recorded, and Lapis has never told anybody as far as I know. All anybody knows is that he bound himself to her and her line until such a time as you release him."

That didn't sit well with me.

He held up a hand. "Before you say anything, I already know how you feel. I never discussed it with either your father or Lapis, but I get the feeling he serves at his own will even if he technically has to do it. His clan is another matter, though, and gargoyles are odd creatures. We're getting ready to head into a war, and we're having enough problems gathering factions and determining who's on our side and who isn't. Now is not the time to take your finger off the scale. Your ancestor worked that deal for a reason, and so did Lapis. The coven hadn't created the stone yet, so victory was pretty much a pipe dream, and Morgana didn't have much to bargain with.

Don't go assuming the legend is accurate and the deal was forced on him."

I nodded. Ring or not, Ronan was my advisor, and my dad had told me to trust him. That's what I was going to do, but I'd also be having a conversation with Lapis.

Motion in the sky as we got within a quarter-mile of where we were going caught my eye, and I leaned forward to look out the windshield. "Is that him?"

Ronan leaned forward to see what I was looking at. "Yep. That's what you signed up for."

His knuckles gripped the wheel, and as I watched Lapis do loops and corkscrew dives, I fought the urge to throw up. Heights weren't my thing, so the only reason I wasn't clawing my way under the seat was because I knew Ronan wouldn't go along with this if I did. Plus, despite my personal fears, I knew it would be foolish to skip gaining this advantage.

Lapis stuck the landing when he flew down to greet us, and it didn't look too jarring. "Ready for your lesson? I was just gettin' warmed up."

I swallowed, or at least I tried to, even though my mouth felt like it was full of cotton. "I'm going to tell you right up front that I hate heights, and I throw up on any carnival ride that goes upside down."

He laughed, though it sounded like a phlegmy cough. "Strictly speaking, those were battle maneuvers I was doing, but I don't think we'll make it that far today. We're just going for a nice smooth ride to get used to it, Mistress."

That made me feel a little better. "You don't have to call me Mistress. Jules will do just fine."

He tilted his head, studying me. "You're the Mistress of Balance. Titles have power, and though you may have close advisors, you should never let them, or anyone else, forget you're the one ultimately in charge. Demand respect when necessary, and take it when it's freely offered to you ... Mistress."

Oddly, that made sense to me. After all, how many times had the phrase "because I'm your mother" crossed my lips?

Though I didn't want to break the moment, I had to ask. "But as a parrot, you called me a couple not-so-respectful names."

I had a feeling he'd have blushed if he could. "I didn't know who you were."

"Does this mean you're gonna stop stealing my bagels?"

He studied me for a moment. "Probably not. But I'll make sure nobody disrespects you or kills you in battle if I can help it."

I blinked. Ronan was right. Gargoyles were weird.

Without another word, he knelt so that I could climb on and begin the most terrifying experience of my life. He was true to his promise to take it easy, though, and after fifteen minutes or so of gentle dips and climbs, I was comfortable enough to leave my eyes open. He skimmed across a body of water, sweeping so low that his toes almost touched it before climbing back into the sky.

At first, he warned me when he was going to turn or change altitude, but soon I began to get the rhythm of it. There was a notch between his wings and shoulders that created a perfect spot for my knees to grip. I found myself enjoying flight, at least until Lapis decided it was time to turn up the volume.

"Okay, Mistress," he called over his shoulder loud enough for me to hear over the wind. "Kiddie ride's over. Put your arms around my neck and hold on. We're going up."

That was all the warning I got. I don't exactly have cat-like reflexes, but when I'm so high in the air that full-grown oak trees look small, I pay attention. I barely had time to do as he said before Lapis took an upward turn that would have made any roller coaster designer proud.

I screamed and squeezed my eyes shut as gravity took hold and tried to rip me from his back. "Are you trying to fucking kill me?" I shrieked, scrambling to maintain my hold as gravity ripped at my body.

"Focus on your center of gravity and where we connect," he called, unperturbed. "Open your mind so you can sense my intentions. I won't let you fall, but I need you to do your part so I can focus on the enemy."

He leveled out, and I tried to calm my mind so I could connect to his. A strange, foreign energy tickled the edges of my consciousness, and I somehow knew we were getting ready to bank right a few seconds before I felt the shift in the powerful muscles beneath me. I'd ridden horses as a kid, and some of that muscle memory came back to me. I adjusted my center of gravity in anticipation.

"Very good, Mistress!"

I could sense pride in his voice, and though some part of my brain was proud of myself, the rest was still trying to recover from the near-death experience.

We did a few more banks and twists before he headed back toward the truck.

When he landed a few feet from Ronan, I was a little disappointed. I climbed off, sure I was grinning like a kid who had just gotten off a roller coaster.

"That was excellent for your first time," Lapis said, smiling, and I preened a little at the approval in his tone.

Ronan raised an eyebrow. "Fabulous. Then she won't need to repeat it."

I shook my head, smiling at Lapis but pretending Ronan hadn't said a word. "Thank you for the lesson. Maybe we can do a few of the more advanced ones next time."

"Maybe so. It would be nice for you not to die in battle. Your father hated cream cheese."

With that, he turned and flew away, leaving me wondering what went on in his mind.

Chapter Twenty-Two

Ronan was chatty as we pulled away, a complete three-sixty from what he'd been on the ride there. I hated to ask, but I had to know what had caused the shift.

He shrugged. "Riding a gargoyle is a skill few master even if they are granted the privilege. I was terrified for you, but you took to it, as you'd say, like a duck to water. Lapis was an excellent teacher, and I feel bad for doubting him."

"He was. To be honest, I had my doubts too. I'm glad we did it, though. Now I'll have another option if this whole mess blows up and we end up in a magical knife fight."

I stretched my back and rolled my head on my shoulders to work out some of the tension. Even though I'd enjoyed the ride after I'd gotten into the rhythm, that didn't mean there was a single point in time when I wasn't hanging on for dear life, and the aerial acrobatics at the end had added new muscle tweaks to the ones I already had from practicing so hard all week. My worst aches and pains had mostly gone away, but my whole body was protesting the sudden abuse. The single best gifts the house had given me were the bottle of Advil and the Jacuzzi tub.

Ronan frowned. "Did he whip you too sharply or bang you around?"

I shook my head. "No, actually, he made the ride as smooth as possible for the most part. I wasn't lying when I said I had a good time, at least after I settled in."

"Battling from atop a gargoyle may be a necessity, but it's unnatural," he said, his tone snooty.

I let that sink in for a few minutes, then laughed at the absurdity of it. "And yet you're offering to let me ride a wolf."

"What? Wolves are graceful creatures. Gargoyles are just giant bats."

My humor must've been contagious because he dropped the façade and started laughing too.

For some reason, the image of Lapis hanging upside down with a bagel hanging out of his mouth formed in my head, and when I combined that with his gravelly tone and odd combination of respect and disregard, I just lost it. Some part of me knew it wasn't really that funny, but I wrote it off as mild hysterics caused by the events of the last few weeks. They say everybody has their breaking point, and maybe I'd finally hit mine.

The great thing was that even though I realized I was getting slaphappy, Ronan laughed along with me when I described the image to him.

When the levity died down, I reached over on a whim and took his hand. I wasn't one of those petite women with tiny hands, but his swallowed mine. I gave it a squeeze and smiled.

He pulled the truck off the edge of the small side road and turned to me. "I don't think I've ever met a woman like you. You laugh at the strangest things, but you make me want to laugh too. Even with everything that's been thrown at you, you've managed to adapt. You have the heart of a wolf."

I realized that was the greatest compliment he could give me. I leaned across the console and he met me halfway, pausing just before he kissed me to nuzzle my nose with his. He slid his hand to the back of my neck and touched his lips to mine. This was different than it had been yesterday. There was no urgency. The kiss was slow and languorous, just his lips moving against mine. A slow burn started in my center and moved outward as I placed my hand on his chest, then slid it up around his neck.

He smiled against my mouth, nuzzled my nose one more time, then pulled away, put the truck back in gear, and drove off. When we came to the main road, he took a right instead of the left that would lead us back to the bar.

"Where are we going?"

"You'll see." He glanced sideways at me, his eyes gray and stormy. Heat crackled between us, stealing my breath, and when he pulled into a driveway a few moments later, I felt like every nerve in my body was on fire.

The drive led to a gorgeous A-frame house, and he wasted no time getting out of the truck and rushing around to open the door for me. Taking my hand as I stepped out, he led me up the front steps, then fumbled with the key to unlock the door. As soon as we were inside, he pushed the door shut, then took my other hand in his. Lacing our fingers together, he lifted my hands above my head and pushed me gently against the door before his mouth crashed down on mine.

I let go of his hands and slipped my arms around his neck, pulling his head down closer and molding my body to his. I'd never experienced anything like the frantic hunger we shared, and I wanted more. He slid his hands down my hips, then stooped and lifted me up as if I weighed nothing. I wrapped my legs around his hips as he turned and carried me down the hallway and into the bedroom. I didn't know what this fire was that burned between us, but I didn't think I'd ever get enough.

* * *

An hour later, we lay spooned together as our breathing slowed and our heart rates returned to normal.

I pulled in a deep breath and blew it slowly out. "Wow."

He tightened his arm around my rib cage and pulled me a little closer, then nuzzled my neck. "Wow, yourself. You're like a drug to me. When we're together, all I want to do is get you in bed. When we're apart, all I want to do is see you."

I wiggled my hips back into him and hummed my agreement. "I don't know what this is between us, but it consumes me. You make me feel valued."

He slid a little bit away from me so that I rolled over on my back, then gazed down into my eyes, his expression intent. "I do value you. It makes me a little sad that you can't see yourself the way I do."

I ran my hand over his shoulder and down the thick, corded muscles of his arm, feeling both feminine and powerful as he stirred against my leg. "In these times, when you look at me like that, I do."

My phone rang, breaking the spell. I smiled at the turn of phrase and gave him a quick kiss before I rolled over to pull it from the back pocket of my shorts lying on the floor.

He ran his hands down my back. "Is it important?"

I glanced at him over my shoulder. "It's CiCi and Laurel. I haven't talked to them in a few days, so if I don't answer, they might just send out a search party."

I scrambled to slip on my tank top and shorts and sat back down the edge of the bed, sliding to answer the call as I did. I angled myself so that they didn't have the same amazing view of Ronan that I did. What I couldn't hide was the goofy grin plastered on my face.

"Hey, Jules," CiCi said with a million-watt smile. "We haven't heard from you in a couple days, so we figured we'd better call and check."

As much as I wanted to tell them about the amazing things I'd been doing, I couldn't. I wanted to tell them I could make storms and pull water from the ocean and turn pottery into sand without even touching it, but I had to keep that to myself.

"I've just been hanging out, learning my way around the bar and spending a lot of time on the beach."

Laurel moved the phone closer to her face and squinted. "Make sure you're wearing sunscreen. Your face looks really pink to me."

That, of course, made me blush even more. I was much more willing to let her believe I was sunburned than flushed from having just finished one of the most incredible rounds of sex I'd ever had. "Yeah, maybe I should apply it more often."

They chatted on a few minutes, and Ronan grinned. Sliding closer to me but being careful to remain out of sight, he slid his finger up my thigh and under the leg of my shorts. I switched hands with my phone and swatted at his arm while doing my best to maintain an interested expression for the girls. In truth, I was interested. I missed them something fierce, but the timing of their call could have been better. I let them chatter for a few minutes, but Ronan was intent on tormenting me, his luscious lips turned up into a wicked grin.

CiCi's next statement was like a bucket of ice water over my head.

"We just booked our plane tickets to come down next weekend, so arrange your schedule so you're free. That is, if you can. If not, we'll get to see you in your new element."

I swallowed. It was entirely possible that we'd be embroiled in some magical power grab for the keys to the universe, and the bar might be ground zero. We were hoping to take the battle to them, but it wasn't like we could pick the time.

"Are you sure about that? Isn't this the busy time for you, Laurel?"

She was a CPA, and the end of a quarter was always busy for her. Technically, it was past that, but I was digging for any rational excuse I could find to keep them away.

"Nope. I cleared my schedule Friday through Tuesday, so get ready. It's time for a girls' weekend at the beach."

I sighed, though I didn't let them see it. I didn't want them to interpret my hesitance as a lack of desire to see them.

I reached for a smile and managed to pull it off. "Sounds great to me. I can't wait to see you guys. I'm so excited!"

That much was true. I really did want to see them, but I also didn't want them to die horrible deaths in some magical war they didn't even know existed.

We wound up the call, and when I disconnected, I pivoted toward Ronan. "What are we gonna do?"

He lifted a bare shoulder. "Right now, you're gonna get back in the moment and let me entertain you. As for your friends, it's time we go on the offensive. We're just gonna have to take the fight to Drake."

I wasn't so confident about the latter, but I was definitely down for the former. I flipped my phone onto the nightstand, then turned my attention back to Ronan. We didn't have much more time because I needed to get back to training, but I figured one more hour wouldn't hurt.

Chapter Twenty-Three

Janelle still hadn't called by the next morning, which didn't go far toward making her look innocent. I prided myself on being a good judge of character, but maybe I was off my game. Since I planned to use the truth-telling spell but didn't feel right using it on an unsuspecting victim, Ronan agreed to be my guinea pig. After all, we had no clue whether it was single use or had a time duration, and if it was for a certain time, we needed to know how long it lasted.

I asked in advance if there was anything he wanted me to avoid because I didn't want to accidentally kick a hornet's nest or hit a nerve. I was a little surprised when he told me I could ask anything I wanted.

"Anything? Are you sure about that?" I asked with a wicked smile.

He grinned back. "I'm an open book. Take your best shot."

I said the spell, doing my best to infuse it with magic.

I could have used it as an excellent opportunity to drag out his deep dark secrets, but I took mercy and asked him standard questions about his life. I did pull his age out of him though; he was in his sixties, which felt really weird to me, but I'd been afraid he was way older than that, so I was overall okay with it.

While we were relaxing on my deck afterwards, Lapis volunteered to let me try it on him to see if it worked on multiple species. I was dying to ask him about his deal with Morgana, but I figured that would be crossing a line since he hadn't shared it with anybody in centuries. Still, I did need to ask tough questions he wouldn't normally answer.

"If you could leave my service, would you?"

He remained quiet for so long that I thought maybe he wasn't going to answer. If he had the ability to refuse, that made the spell a lot less effective.

After almost a minute, his stone lips curved into an appreciative smile. "You are the first heir to ask me that question even though it's fundamental to our relationship. Each of your ancestors assumed I relinquished my freedom and gave blind loyalty to her and her line. Gargoyles are a proud species, and nothing she could have offered or threatened would have been enough to make me forfeit my soul. I am bound to you, but there are provisions. We took five days to craft that spell because it wasn't an accord that either of us entered lightly."

I debated pressing him for more details, but he'd obviously crafted his response so that he answered the question without giving out information he didn't want me to have. That was something to keep in mind for the future, but not a tool I was willing to abuse. Satisfied that I'd tested the spell and learned its parameters, I leaned back in my chair, lacing my fingers across my midriff.

The spell worked like a charm, pardon the cliché, except an hour and a half later, they were still bewitched.

Since I had zero clue what to do in such a situation, I asked Ronan what he thought we should do.

Unfortunately, the truth spell was working a little too well. He opened his mouth and began reciting a laundry list of what he wanted to do the next time he caught me alone.

Lapis, currently in his gargoyle form, let out a raspy snicker, and I ran my tongue over my teeth, trying to suppress my grin. Ronan was blushing like a teenager at his first dance while explicitly reciting sexy-time activities so creative I had to wonder if some of them were even physically possible.

I held up a hand to stop him before he dragged me down the erotic rabbit hole with him. "Asked and answered. Let me rephrase that. What should we do about ending this spell? It's perfectly fine for you to be brutally honest with me, but it would be a terrible idea for you to go down to the bar or anywhere else in public like this."

Ronan kept his mouth clamped shut as he hunched in his deck chair and stared out over the ocean.

"Normally, I'd let you figure this out on your own for the experience," Lapis said, "but your learning curve is steep, and time is limited. I suggest checking the book; so far, it's given you a solution every time you've needed one."

I was a little annoyed I hadn't thought of that, but in my defense, I'd only been at it for a week and a half.

As Lapis had predicted, the book provided the counter spell. I had to wonder why it didn't give it to me along with the original spell, but that was at the bottom of the list of things I didn't understand in my new life.

Ronan's phone rang, and when he saw who was calling, he frowned.

"Hey, Mom," he said when he slid to answer. "Any more news?"

He listened for a moment, frowning. "I'm going to put you on speaker. Jules and Lapis are here, and it'll just be easier if you tell us all at once."

He tapped the screen of his phone. "Okay, go ahead."

"Hi, Jules," she said. "It's nice to sort of meet you, though I wish it were under more pleasant circumstances."

"The pleasure is mine," I replied. "And I couldn't agree more."

Lapis cleared his throat. "Go ahead, Alexa. We are all listening. What's the latest news?"

"I'm afraid it's worse than we thought," she replied. "I've been doing a little more digging, and we have at least twenty top-tier witches and wizards missing. Some of them were solo practitioners and recluses, so nobody noticed their absence until we started looking."

I blew out a breath, puffing my cheeks. "Is it possible at least some of them are just somewhere off the grid?"

She paused for a second. "I suppose that could be the case for a few of them, but I don't put a lot of stock in coincidence. Especially now."

Lapis shook his head. "There's no such thing as coincidence. Not in times like this. I'll reach out to my clan and make it clear whose side we're on. In the meantime, I think we should double up Jules's training. It's not ideal for her to skip steps, but I think we need to switch to offensive training using what skills she's already learned."

"I couldn't agree more," she replied. "In fact, I'm getting on a plane in just a few minutes, and I'll be there tomorrow morning. I believe I can help because I've researched that necklace and the history of her line probably more than anybody else has. I have a good idea of what she can do, and I'm also in a better position to help her use her strengths to overcome her physical weakness."

Since that was one of my greatest concerns and something I considered a hole in my training, I sighed in relief. "Thank you. You have no idea how much I appreciate that."

"I consider it an honor. The stronger we are individually, the stronger we'll be as a group. Since you are potentially our strongest asset, we need you as close to full strength as we can get you."

I did my best not to let that scare the shit out of me. I was used to being in a leadership role, but up to this point in my life, the stakes had been nothing compared to now.

We made arrangements to pick her up at the airport, then ended the call. Even knowing she was coming took a huge weight off my shoulders. Now to find the ring.

The phone call hadn't helped the sense of urgency that was pressing me to constantly move, move, move. I stood from my chair and paced on the deck, my palms pressed against my temples.

"I haven't learned enough. I'm not ready to go up against some guy who's known this stuff all his life. Somebody who doesn't even hesitate to kill people. I'm a freakin' soccer mom, for God's sake. My skill set is herding kids and schmoozing clients. The craziest thing I've done in twenty years is wear my days-of-the-week undies out of order."

"Jules!" Ronan stepped in front of me and put his hands on my forearms, stopping me. "Look around. Is this something a weak woman would do?"

With effort, I pulled out of my own head and looked around, chest heaving. The clay pots situated around the deck hovered, quivering, several feet in the air, and the vines planted in the hanging baskets had grown to three times their original size. I pulled in a deep, steadying breath, and focused on gently lowering the pots and drawing my magic back into myself.

"You gotta get a handle on that," Lapis grunted. "What are you gonna do the next time somebody steals your parking space at the grocery store or gets in your face one night in the bar?"

I flopped back down in my chair and dropped my head in my hands. "See? I can't even control myself enough to keep shit from goin' full-on crazy when I have a little meltdown in my own home. How am I ever gonna manage it when it really matters?"

Ronan knelt in front of me and tilted my chin up so that I had to look at him. "You're missing the point. You're much more than just a soccer mom. That was just one thing you were really good at. It's not who you are. You're Jules Cavanaugh. You've survived childbirth--twice—and managed to get both of those kids to adulthood. You kept them alive when they were too small to protect themselves, and you didn't kill them when they no doubt pressed every single button you have when they were teenagers. You survived an unfaithful husband by scrawling a note on the back of a utility bill and moved almost six hundred miles away to start over in a new place, sight unseen. In less than two weeks, you've learned more about magic than most people learn in a decade, you already have some amazing people firmly in your corner. You're more powerful than you know, both as a person and as the Mistress of Balance."

I glanced from him to Lapis, who perched on the railing in his parrot form. He shrugged. "Don't look at me. Motivational speeches are not my thing. I will say, though, that I've already notified my clan to be on standby to follow you into battle."

While all those things Ronan had said were great, Lapis's willingness to put his life and the lives of his family in my hands was both incredibly humbling and terrifying.

Still, if he didn't have absolute faith in me, I knew he wouldn't have done it, bond or no.

My phone rang, bringing me back to earth. I slid it across the table and glanced at the screen. "It's Janelle. What should I say?"

Lapis scoffed. "You tell her whatever you have to to get her over here. We need to find out whether or not she took that ring. If she did, we need to get it back. If she didn't, we need to keep looking. That's our top priority right now."

Pulling in one last steadying breath, I answered the phone. I didn't have any problem getting her to agree to drinks on my balcony. That made me wonder if she was innocent or just cocky. Whichever it was, I'd have my chance to find out in less than five minutes. She was already down at the bar.

"Hey," she said, looking around when I opened the door for her. "This place is great. I hadn't even realized there was an apartment up here until you told me about it. I just assumed it was all storage."

She wandered around, examining the exposed beams and looking at the pictures on the wall. "You've done a great job decorating it."

Rather than tell her the house magically decorated itself for me, I just smiled and thanked her.

Ronan popped the cork on a bottle of red and poured us each a glass. "Let's take this to the deck if that's all right with everyone."

Once we were settled, she ran her finger around the top of her glass. "What do you need to talk about? You sounded kind of urgent on the phone. Is everything okay?"

I decided to stick as close to the truth as possible, glancing at Ronan and willing him to distract her so I could do the spell. Apparently, that got through to him because he made a show of fumbling his phone out of his lap. While her attention was away, I whispered the words, careful to direct them and my magic toward her. I was getting a pretty good handle on that, at least when I had my emotions under control.

"To be honest, everything isn't all right. I had something stolen from my purse. I was wondering if you noticed anybody at all messing with it at any point."

I hoped I'd phrased it well enough so that she was included in that.

She thought for a minute and shook her head. "No. Had I seen anybody messing with it, I would have stopped them."

I licked my lips and took a drink of my wine to buy time to think of another question. "Do you know anybody by the name of Drake?"

She pressed her lips together and shook her head. "Other than the musician, no. Why? Do you think maybe he's the one that stole from you? What are you missing, anyway?"

I sighed, then glanced at Ronan, who shrugged.

"Some jewelry my father left me, and I really need to get it back. It's important to me."

Ronan stood. "It's a shame we don't have some way to magically detect when bad people come in the bar. It doesn't happen often, but this isn't the first time we've had stuff come up missing from the bar." He cast a meaningful glance my direction. "I think we have some cheese and crackers. I'll go get them."

I caught his hint. When he brought the cheese plate back out, it would give me the distraction I'd need to cast the magic detection spell. There had to be some way to do this type of magic without using words. I hadn't needed any words when I summoned a hurricane, so there had to be a way to use spells this simple without saying them out loud.

He was only gone a couple minutes, and when he returned with a cheese plate and paper plates, I wondered if the apartment magically whipped it up or if he'd brought it himself. I didn't even remember buying cheese. While he fussed over distributing the plates, I did what I needed to do, then waited for something to happen. A lavender haze outlined Ronan, but nothing happened with the other two. I furrowed my brow, wondering if I'd done it wrong. Since Janelle thanked him, then reached for a couple crackers and a slice of cheddar, I had to assume she couldn't see the outline. A heartbeat later, a pink haze surrounded her, and my pulse raced. I didn't know what to make of the colors, but I had to assume if something happened, it would mean she had some sort of magic. What threw me, though, was that nothing appeared around Lapis. A few seconds later, the auras around Ronan and Janelle disappeared, leaving me with more questions than answers.

"You said you moved here from Maine, right? Tell me about it. I've never been."

I thought maybe it was a good idea to get some background information from her. If Ronan's mom was as good at researching as he claimed, she might be able to do something with the information. She'd told me all about her ex-husband, so I already had that to give to Alexa.

Janelle chattered on for a while, and it was obvious from the way her face lit up that she'd loved her old home. Since we couldn't just boot her out, we spent the next half hour chatting about the Dolphin Key area and about some of the places she had for sale. When she finished her second glass of wine, she glanced at the clock on her phone.

"I hate to run, but I promised a client I'd meet him for

dinner. If I sit here and have another glass of wine, I won't be able to leave this balcony, let alone the property. I hope you get your jewelry back, and I'll keep an eye out for anybody shady. You might want to check the local pawn shops. If it was just somebody looking for cash, they might've ditched it there."

After she was gone, Ronan turned to me, brows up. "Well?"

I turned my hand palm up. "Well, she did have a reaction to the spell, but I'm not sure I did it right, though. You had a purple outline, but Lapis had nothing. Yours was purple, but Janelle's was pink."

"You probably did it right," Lapis replied. "Technically, I have no magic."

I tilted my head at him. "But you can fly. And you're a gargoyle."

He laughed. "I fly because I have wings. There's nothing magical about that. As far as being a gargoyle, there's nothing really magical about that, either, at least not for the purposes of the spell. I am what I was born to be."

The lines between what I'd always known was fact and what I'd always believed was fantasy had blurred to the point that they were nonexistent. Rather than try to unpack all that, I just slugged my wine, kicked up my feet, and enjoyed the sunset while I could.

Chapter Twenty-Four

We picked Alexa up at seven o'clock the next morning. For some reason, I'd expected her to be a tiny brunette. I had the hair right, but she was my height—five-six. That was where our similarities ended, though. She was built like an Amazonian warrior and had fewer wrinkles than I did even though she was a generation ahead of me. The whole werewolf-aging thing looked good on her, but it didn't do much for my baggy-eyed ego.

I recognized her as soon as she stepped off the airplane because even though their hair color differed, Ronan had obviously gotten his eyes and facial features from her. Confidence oozed from her very pores, and she was one of the most graceful people I'd ever seen.

Ronan scooped her into a hug, and she pushed him back to arm's length. "Let me look at you. It's been way too long. I know you love it over here, but it wouldn't kill you to come home more often."

I smiled at the motherly affection even as a little stab of

sadness pierced my heart. That was exactly something my mother would've said.

"And you must be Jules." Instead of offering her hand, she pulled me into a hug too. "This all has to be so overwhelming for you, but don't worry. We'll have you whipped into shape in no time."

My aching muscles groaned in protest at just the thought, but I returned her smile. "I sure hope you're right. I feel like I'm behind the eight ball here."

She laughed as Ronan picked up her suitcase. "Sweetie, we all feel that way right now. You are not rowing this boat alone. Now, let's get somewhere we can talk openly."

She didn't waste any time once we were in the truck. "Bring me up to speed. What exactly have you learned to do, and have you found any particular areas of strength?"

I ran through the laundry list of skills I'd been developing. "I can work with all the elements, but air and earth come easier. I'm still working on learning to control fire, and water is a real struggle."

Ronan laughed, then told her about my disaster on my first day. "I wish you could've seen it. We heard her scream, and when we got there, she had fire shooting out of her hand and was shaking it, trying to put it out. She had the entire room on fire before Erik could dampen her magic."

I blushed, embarrassed, but had to admit that the way he framed it painted a funny picture when I envisioned it from his eyes.

He stuck his tongue in his cheek and then grinned. "There's also a sock stuck in her wall. Apparently, her house has a mocking sense of humor."

She patted me on the shoulder, her eyes alight. "Don't worry. If that's the worst you did, you're way ahead of most witches, even if you are a couple of decades late to the game. Even summoning fire takes most witches years to manage if they ever do. That bodes well for us."

She turned to Ronan. "There's no need to take me to your place. We can drop the luggage off later, and I'd like to get started as soon as we can. Let's go straight to the warehouse."

Though I knew in my heart we didn't have any time to waste, I'd hoped for at least an hour's reprieve, both to give the Advil a chance to kick in and to get used to her before she put me through my magical paces. She was right, though. We'd have time to relax and get to know each other after we dealt with Drake. For now, getting me ready to do that was a top priority.

Three hours later, sweat dripped off the tip of my nose and onto the gymnastics mat beneath my feet as I bent over, my hands braced on my knees. My entire body was shaking, and I felt like somebody had taken a ball bat to me. It hadn't taken Alexa long to put me through a few magical drills before she'd nodded in approval and insisted on moving to the hand-to-hand drills. She'd spent the last hour and a half kicking my ass.

"Again," she said, her hands resting on her hips in a tone exactly matching Ronan's. At least I knew now where he'd gotten it.

I pressed against the stitch in my side. "I don't think I can. I'm not trying to be a baby or quitter, but I don't think I can physically do another round."

A frown line appeared between her eyes. "Maybe we should focus more on your magic for now. Time is limited, and physical strength takes months to build up. We don't have that kind of time, so we need to put our efforts where we can get the most results."

I was so relieved I could have cried, but there was no

way I was breaking down in tears in front of this incredible woman. I sucked down half a bottle of water, and my stomach growled.

She arched a perfect brow. "Have you burned through your breakfast already, or did you guys not take the time to eat before you picked me up?"

I shook my head as I dabbed the sweat off my forehead with my towel. "We overslept and barely had time to grab coffee on our way out the door."

That wasn't entirely the truth. We'd woken up in plenty of time, but Ronan had distracted me in the most pleasant of ways in the shower. My face warmed just thinking about it, especially considering this was his mother.

She laughed, a knowing expression on her face. "Love may slake one appetite, but it increases the other. Let's go get some lunch."

I glanced at Ronan, who'd mostly stood back and watched the drills, and was surprised to see he was grinning from ear to ear.

He shrugged, obviously picking up on my embarrassment. "I told you shifters were virile. That extends to the women too."

One side of his mother's mouth curved into a half-smile as she gathered our stuff. "A healthy sex life makes for a healthy relationship. It's normal and natural and something to be proud of. I've never understood why humans insist on making it into something borderline shameful."

Unsure how to respond, I just stuffed my towel in my duffel bag and zipped it up. Though I agreed with the philosophy, a lifetime of social training was hard to overcome.

Ronan took us to Bubba's Burgers, which had become our go-to place on training days. With the way I'd been pounding down food, I was shocked my butt wasn't as wide as a barn. In fact, when I'd weighed myself the day before, I'd lost two pounds. A normal person would have probably lost ten with all the physical activity I'd been doing, but I was taking the win.

Alexa took a long pull from her strawberry milkshake and pulled a file folder from her bag. "I've been researching your line because Ronan told me you didn't know anything about it. Though I'm sure your father's intentions were good, they were selfish. Your grandmother was fortunate to live in a time of peace, but she did carry out her duties on the rare occasions when they were necessary, and she stayed in top form until the day she died of old age." She smiled at me. "You'll be happy to know she lived almost two hundred years, and if I did my math correctly, your dad was sixty when you were born."

That flabbergasted me. When he'd left, he'd taken all the pictures of himself except for one that my mother later found on a roll of old film. He hadn't looked a day over thirty-five. That meant he'd been over a hundred when he'd died, and my brain almost broke contemplating that. Even in the bar pictures I'd found in the album, he'd only looked sixty-ish.

I thought about what the effects of gravity and years had already done to me. "What's that mean for me, though? I obviously haven't enjoyed that perk."

She tilted her head, reminding me of a bird. "I can't say for sure, but my guess would be that now that you've claimed your magic, that's going to slow down a bit."

I wasn't as disappointed as I should've been, which was weird. Over the last few weeks, I'd grown much more comfortable in my own skin. I attributed a lot of that to the fact that Ronan seemed to like me just the way I was. Of course, the magic had taken care of the major aches and pains, so that helped too. Still, I was happy to know my golden years were quite a bit farther in my future than they had been just a month ago.

I popped a french fry in my mouth. "I'm okay with that. How long do shifters live?"

As soon as I asked it, I felt a little like I'd overstepped. That seemed like a personal question, but neither Alexa nor Ronan seemed bothered by it.

Ronan lifted a shoulder, then washed a bite of cheeseburger down with his tea. "Just like witches, it varies from pack to pack. Ours seems to have about the same lifespan your line does."

As they sat side-by-side, I was surprised to notice that she shared some of the same tattoos that Ronan had on his upper arm. Since they'd both been open about other personal questions, I figured it wouldn't hurt to ask about them. "Ronan told me there was a story behind those runes on his arm, and you have the same ones. Is it too forward of me to ask about them?"

She raised her brows. "Of course not. It's common knowledge to most magical people. The ones we share, we were born with. Some of his, he also inherited from his father. They're sort of hard to explain, but they're a combination of protective symbols and genealogy. He's added several to the ones he was born with, though. Some are magical, and others are just for decoration. He seems to think he's a human canvas. Ask to see his Marvin the Martian."

I opened my mouth to ask because it sounded like a story waiting to be told, but the same tide of anger and resentment that had hit me in the bar slammed into me almost like a physical attack. I stiffened and dropped my burger into the basket. Ronan had apparently felt it too, because he whipped his head up and scanned the room, his expression fierce.

"Are you getting that?" Like him, I examined every face in the place looking for the source.

"Getting what?" Alexa asked, though she began to scan the crowd as well. I assumed that came from a lifetime spent as a pack member. She might not have picked up on the danger firsthand, but she had sensed the alarm rolling off Ronan, and maybe me too.

"It's the same negative emotions I told you she picked up in the bar." Ronan's posture had gone from relaxed to tense and ready to do battle. The change in his demeanor wasn't just physical, either. The air around him crackled with danger, and though I'd experienced the alpha side of him during sex, this was something different. Even knowing he was on my side, my fight-or-flight instinct kicked in, and flight won, hands down. This man was dangerous and ready to defend the two people he perceived as under his protection. The same energy rolled off his mother, and I understood for the first time exactly how formidable these two beings were.

Despite the onslaught of emotion continuing, not a single person in the place appeared to be the one responsible. Just like at the bar, nobody was staring at us, and everybody seemed to be having a good time. I did another scan, this time focusing on faces and hoping I recognized somebody.

Ronan growled in frustration and slammed his hand down on the table so hard that several people turned to stare at us.

Alexa placed her hand on his arm. "We need to leave.

We can't start something in front of all these people, and it's not ideal for defense, either."

Ronan gave a sharp nod and stood up, not taking his eyes off the crowd. I did my best to convey to the other diners that all was well by smiling at them, but I had a feeling that fell flat considering the energy rolling off Ronan. He took me by the hand, but rather than lead me toward the door, he nudged me so that I walked in front of him, and he never turned his back to the crowd. Alexa, on the other hand led the way toward the door, sandwiching me between the two of them as she focused on any danger that might lie in wait outside.

We were halfway home before the tension in the air started to subside.

"What the hell was that?" Alexa asked, her expression fierce. "I didn't feel a thing, and from the vibes you two were throwing off, that concerns me more than a little."

I shrugged and turned my palm upward helplessly. "It's just this disjointed wall of rage and disgust. I can never tell where it's coming from, and I don't think I recognized anybody in the restaurant from the bar."

She pulled in a deep breath and blew it out through pursed lips, obviously trying to regain her equilibrium."We need to shore up security. This is no coincidence, and it would be foolish not to close ranks."

Ronan nodded. Though most of the aggression had subsided from his energy, he remained physically vigilant. "I agree, and we need to call our meeting of the clans and covens."

"I'll make the calls as soon as we get home," Alexa replied. "I'll set up a conference call for this afternoon."

Despite the gravity of the situation, I smiled. Even magic was fast tracked by the wonders of technology.

Chapter Twenty-Five

We didn't even stop by Ronan's house to drop off Alexa's luggage. Though she'd taken a red-eye flight, she didn't seem to be suffering from jet lag, exhaustion, or any of the other issues I'd have been dealing with. She was either the Energizer Bunny in disguise or crazy good at hiding how she really felt. Something told me it was the former.

As soon as we got back to the bar, I took them straight to my apartment, where both of them dove straight into making phone calls. Feeling a little useless, I straightened up the house, then got out the book. Hopefully, it had given me some new spells because I had a feeling I was going to need all the help I could get, and soon. It bugged me that somebody could foster the level of emotions this person was without any outward display. Anybody who could hide their emotions like that had to be at least a little unstable if only because hate on that level ate away at your soul.

An hour later, Alexa hung up her phone, and rather than search through her contacts and make another call, she stuffed it in her back pocket. "Everything's set. I activated the network and put the word out that we'll be meeting via conference call at seven."

Ronan nodded. "I touched base with our clan leaders and put them on alert. They were already together for training drills, so we're good to go. The only thing we need to figure out is where Drake is. Then we can take the fight to him."

Something Alexa had said caught my attention. "What do you mean when you say you activated the network? All I can picture in my head is my PTA phone tree."

She smiled. "That's accurate. There's no way anyone of us could make contact with everybody in an emergency in time to be effective, so we organized a network. Each person in the network is responsible for calling five people, and it trickles down. Doing it that way, we can have everybody on board and up to speed in less than an hour."

That shocked me, mainly because there was always at least one person in the network who didn't get with the program. I said as much.

She rubbed her chin, and the corners of her eyes crinkled with wry humor. "Yeah, we don't have that problem. Participation isn't optional, and consequences of not following through are harsh. Trust me, by the time seven o'clock rolls around, every single person in the network will not only be informed, they'll have done their research so they can share anything relevant in their region. They'll drop whatever they're doing to join the call."

That was impressive though I shuddered to think what those consequences might be.

Ronan motioned toward the book. "Did it give you anything new?"

I nodded. "It did, but none of it makes a whole lot of sense to me. Well, a couple do because they involve increasing communication with my advisor. That's the term the book used, but I'm not sure how effective the spell will be without the ring. It didn't say anything about that part, so I don't know if the book's aware that it's missing."

Alexa sat down beside me. "I admit I'm not completely up to speed on this part yet, but based on the fact that it's giving you spells as you need them, I believe it's safe to assume the book knows. Can I see?"

I nodded and passed it to her.

She scanned the pages, starting at the beginning, so it took her a few minutes to get through the whole thing. When she finished, she chewed on her lip for a minute, thinking. "The one thing about magic is that it's often mysterious. The one thing I believe we can count on is that the book believes you're going to need to master this knowledge sooner rather than later."

Though I'd been hoping she'd tell me something different, that was the conclusion I'd come to as well.

"What's the spell?" Ronan asked. "I don't have the sort of magic it takes to do things like that, so is it just for you?"

I shook my head. "That one isn't so much a spell as it is an exercise. It's targeted at both of us, and the short explanation is that we just need to learn each other's energy and focus on that. Apparently, we can increase the distance the more we get to know each other."

He wobbled his head back and forth. "That sounds like something we won't have too hard of a time mastering. We're already in tune to each other's emotions, and we're exchanging information on a subconscious level, so it sounds like all we need to do is focus on that."

I just loved how he made it sound so easy. Even though I'd lived in a bubble in my old life, I'd typically been the one in charge. I know it sounds arrogant, but I was used to being the smartest person in the room. Or at least the most capable. Since this whole magic thing had started, that had gone out the window. I'd been struggling for two weeks to master skills ten-year-olds apparently had. Granted, my skill set was much broader than theirs typically were, but I still felt inept and even a little bit stupid sometimes. The fact that everybody had such high expectations just added to the stress and frustration.

I put the book on the table with more force than was strictly necessary, then stood and snatched my purse from the counter.

Ronan reached out and took my arm. "Wait. Where you going?"

For a man who claimed to sense my emotions, he was being thick as molasses.

I snatched my arm from him and headed toward the door. "I'm going to go have a glass of wine at the bar. There's nothing I can do here, anyway, and I need a break."

Yes, I realized I was being a bit of a dramatic diva, but if I didn't get some breathing space, I was going to snap. The emotional and physical stress was catching up with me, and I didn't want to take it out on them.

Ronan reached for me again, but Alexa shot me a sympathetic look, then put her hand on his arm and shook her head. "Let her go. We need to strategize, and she needs some space. Give it to her."

Grateful for her intervention, I headed down to the bar. I debated getting in my car and burning off some frustration, but I was mad, not stupid. After all, knowing I was the weak link was at the root of my current issue. Testing fate just because I was in the midst of a mild hissy fit would have been foolish. Instead, I tossed my purse on the bar and climbed onto the stool that I'd come to think of as mine.

"Rough day?" Austin asked as he slid a coaster in front of me.

I rolled my head, willing some of the tension to leave my shoulders. "You have no idea. Can I get a glass of red and a shot of tequila?"

I realized I couldn't get blackout drunk like I really wanted to, but one shot wouldn't kill me and might possibly keep me from going nuclear. I huffed out a humorless laugh when I realized how accurate that turn of phrase was.

Eddie and Erik showed up just as Austin delivered my drinks.

Eddie saw what was in front of me and cringed."Ooh, is it that bad, sugar?"

I slammed the shot and grimaced as I bit the lime. "Oh, no. It's way worse, but I need to keep it between the lines. That's why there's only one shot."

Erik slid onto his stool. "Is Mommy Dearest hideous? Is she being mean to you?"

I shook my head and took a drink of my wine. "No. In fact, she's been great. I'm just worn to the bone, physically and mentally."

Eddie, who'd taken the stool next to me, patted my forearm. "You're putting too much pressure on yourself. There's no rush, and we all just want to help you. However, if that means an afternoon of tequila-induced revelry, then we're all in for that too. Austin, two shots of tequila, and get our girl another one too."

I held up my hand. "I'm not entirely sure that's a great idea."

We hadn't filled the guys in on the whole Drake thing, but I made an executive decision. "Let's go over to the far table. I have something I need to talk to you two about. "

They shared a knowing look, and Cerbi, which I now knew was short for Cerberus, licked my hand.

Erik leaned over Eddie and lowered his voice. "If you're gonna confess you're the Mistress of Balance, we already know."

I blinked a couple times, absorbing that. "Then why didn't you say anything?"

Eddie flapped his hand. "We figured if you wanted us to know, you'd tell us yourself. You've been walking around like you have the weight of the world on your shoulders, and we didn't want to add to that."

I was so grateful to have these guys that I almost cried. Then, I realized that they only had part of the story. Thankfully, the bar was slow, so even though we hadn't moved to the table, nobody would ever hear us.

I leaned in so that we were in a little huddle. "That's just it. I do have the weight of the world on my shoulders."

I filled them in on everything—Drake, the weird sensation of anger without an apparent source, and my own frustration and sense of inadequacy. "So, yeah. Here I am, an empty-nester pushing fifty, and apparently I'm going to have to lead some sort of magical army against the forces of evil who are trying to extinguish good magic." I rolled my eyes and huffed out a breath. "Do you have any idea how crazy that sounds to me? It's the plot to a movie or a fantasy book, not something you actually ever say in real life."

Austin set the shots in front of us, then leaned in. "Not to make your life any harder, but if you're going to talk about this, you really do need to take it over to the table and use a privacy spell."

My head about exploded when the implications of that statement hit me. I put my palm to my forehead. "You too?

What are you? A genie? No, wait. You're a demigod here to make sure I don't blow up the world."

He laughed, and I wanted to reach across and slap him. "Nothing so fancy as that. I'm a wolf shifter just like Ronan. In fact, I'm the second son of one of his clan leaders."

I sighed. Suddenly, that exchange on my second day there made a whole lot more sense. "Is there one single person I've talked to who's actually just what they seem?"

Cerbi licked my hand again, then laid his head against my calf. Despite my earlier resolve to stick with one shot, I picked up the second one and slammed it.

"I think you've managed to dig all the skeletons out of the closet now," Eddie said. "Though I suppose in the interest of full disclosure, I do have a little black box of souls I've collected over the years hidden in my underwear drawer."

I looked at him, trying to decide if he was being serious or just teasing me. Even the fact that I had to consider that was surreal. When he winked at me and smiled, I nudged him with my elbow. "Keep it up, smart-ass. I swear, one more straw is gonna break this camel's back."

Since the front window of my apartment looked out over the bar, I wasn't surprised when I felt watchful eyes. A sense of concern accompanied the feeling, and I recognized Ronan's energy. I glanced toward the window and smiled at him. None of this was his fault, and he was doing everything he could to help me. I didn't want him to think I was mad at him rather than the situation.

I felt like I should be doing anything other than sitting in the bar drinking with friends, but I couldn't for the life of me figure out what. While Ronan and Alexa had been making their phone calls, I'd committed the new spells to memory.

Most of them were easy—summoning light, levitating, and casting the exact privacy bubble that Austin had mentioned. There was also one for creating a physical barrier around myself along with the exercises to communicate more effectively with Ronan.

I'd practiced the first two and memorized the others since there wasn't really a way to test them by myself. Ronan and Alexa were strategizing, whatever that meant, so there was nothing left for me to do until the conference call at seven. Though neither of them had told me I needed to be present for it, I assumed it was implied. For that reason, I had a big glass of water instead of a second glass of wine. The last thing I wanted to do was put in my first appearance drunk.

It wasn't long before I started feeling restless. I hadn't had much downtime since the first couple of days I was there, and I wasn't quite sure what to do with myself.

I pushed off my stool, unable to sit still a moment longer. "I want to take a walk on the beach. I need to clear my head, and the water soothes me. Are you guys going to be here for a minute?"

Eddie shook his head. "No, we have a thing in an hour, so we need to go. But go do your thing, sugar. Take Cerbi with you, though, and keep him for the night. You shouldn't be alone."

"Agreed," Erik said, snapping his fingers. "Cerbi, go with her."

The command hadn't been necessary, though, because the hellhound-slash-puggle had already jumped to his feet when I stood up.

Even though it was hot, the breeze blowing in off the ocean dried the sweat on the back of my neck. At the water's edge, I picked up a stick. Cerbi jumped up and down, trying to take it out of my hand. I tossed it as far as I could and smiled as he bounded after it.

Lapis's consciousness tickled the edge of mine, and I glanced up to see him floating above me so high he was barely a speck. It was nice to know he was there, and I appreciated that he was giving me my space while watching over me. I spent the next ten minutes strolling and tossing the stick for Cerbi.

The beach was quieter than usual, and I was grateful. I didn't feel like dodging Frisbees and listening to screaming children. I smiled when four joggers approached but didn't pay them any mind as I put a little bit of magical oomph into throwing Cerbi's stick. People used that stretch of beach for exercise all the time.

As they approached me, one of them bumped into me, knocking me down. The other reached for my necklace and tried to snatch it off my throat. I reacted automatically by grabbing for my neck and holding it in place. I needn't have bothered, though, because even though the man had yanked it hard enough that it should have broken, all it did was cut into the back of my neck.

I cried out for Cerbi and did my best to call out to Lapis and Ronan through our links while I struggled with the men. Two of them were holding me down while one was trying to get the necklace off of me. I didn't know where the fourth was, and I didn't have time to worry about it.

My initial reaction was one of a human, and it took me a couple of seconds to remember I had magic at my disposal. I summoned it, though for the life of me, none of the spells I'd learned popped into my head.

Instead, I let my instincts take over.

I yanked one arm free and thrust out my hand, electrocuting the man who had his hand to my throat. That blasted him back, giving me the space to jump to my feet. One of the men who'd been holding me came at me, and I brought my elbow up into the side of his face like Alexa had taught me, adding some magical power to it. Primal satisfaction shot through me when I felt a bone crush.

An unearthly snarl sounded from behind me, and Cerberus vaulted into my line of sight in full hellhound form, crashing straight into the guy I'd just hit.

Lapis spiraled through the sky, using his talons to rip through the one I'd shocked before he could get back to me. I turned my efforts to the remaining one who had attacked me. We'd turned so that I was facing the bar, and I sent a little thanks to the universe when I saw Ronan running toward me. Midstride, he shifted from human to a massive, tawny wolf, and I knew this battle was over.

I summoned fire to my hand and blasted the man I was fighting. Victory, magic, and adrenaline pumped through me so that I felt like a freakin' superhero. I'd counted the battle over too soon, though.

The fourth man, whom I'd lost track of, wrapped his arm around my chest from behind me and slammed a hood over my head. The last thing I saw was Ronan bounding toward me across the sand. Something pricked me in the neck, and everything went dark.

Chapter Twenty-Six

I woke tied to a chair, the hood still over my head. I struggled, trying to free my wrists and ankles. The hood was thin enough that a little bit of light filtered through, but not so thin that I could see through it. My heart raced, and a million thoughts ran through my head.

Just breathe, I thought. *Think. You're not some helpless human. You're the fucking Mistress of Balance, for God's sake.*

Pulling in a couple of deep breaths, I willed my heart and my thoughts to slow. I listened and tried to send out tendrils of magic to see if I was alone. I didn't hear anything with either, but I wasn't willing to place a lot of faith in my magic. I'd never tried that before, and if it was going to be a matter of life and death, I wasn't depending on it.

Since I couldn't see or hear anything, I turned to my final sense and pulled in a big breath through my nose. The place smelled musty, and I picked out the faint odors of fish and diesel fuel. Using fire was out, then. The last thing I needed to do was blow myself up.

I turned my attention to my ropes, trying to concentrate

my magic. First, I tried to untie them, then I tried to dissolve them back into their natural form. Neither worked.

I racked my brain, trying to come up with a solution, but my thoughts felt sluggish.

"Hey!" I called. "Is anybody here?"

My voice echoed a little in the room, giving me the sense that I was in a large, open area—a warehouse, maybe.

Nobody answered, though all the murder shows I'd watched had taught me that didn't mean anything. They could be lurking there silently, just waiting for the phone call to kill me. The image of Rob standing by my grave, shaking his head and saying, "I told her so," shot through my brain. I renewed my effort just to spite him and turned my thoughts, instead, to his polar opposite—the man who'd been a supportive, positive presence in my life.

I struggled to remember exactly what the spell book had said about connecting with Ronan, but I drew a blank. I'd only skimmed it, and even using my go-to memory trick of picturing the page, all I could remember was that I was supposed to search for his essence, whatever that meant. Pressure behind my eyes was making it hard to think.

It occurred to me that even if I could reach him, I had no idea where I was at. I didn't know how long I'd been out or how I'd gotten there. I could be ten minutes away from the bar or ten hours. Since the place smelled like fish, I held out hope for the former. I decided to give it a shot, anyway. If nothing else, I could let him know I was okay. I tried to clear my head and search for him, focusing on how his emotions felt in my mind. For a brief moment, I brushed up against his familiar energy, or at least I thought I did.

I growled in frustration. Just feeling him was useless if I couldn't tell him where I was or give him any sort of landmark. I guess if he felt me, it might be some comfort to him because he'd know I was alive, but that was about it. Knowing Ronan, that would drive him mad with frustration.

Next, I reached out to Lapis. Strangely, I connected to him almost immediately and sagged in relief. Even knowing I wasn't alone in my head was a comfort.

His words were plain as day in my mind.

Lapis: *Thank the gods. Where are you? Are you okay? Your energy feels off.*

Me: *Yeah, I'm okay. Just a little fuzzy-headed. I have no idea where I'm at, though. I woke up tied to a chair with a bag over my head. I think it's some sort of warehouse, and it smells musty, like fish and diesel fuel.*

Hopefully, that would be more helpful to him than it was to me.

Lapis: *Fabulous. You just described every warehouse in every beach town everywhere. Keep our link open. Ronan thought he sensed you a minute ago and about lost his mind. I'll let him know you're okay, I'll try to get a bead on the necklace.*

So that was it. We were linked because he was pledged to my line, and the necklace facilitated that. It was good information to have, assuming I didn't die before he could find me.

I shoved that defeatist thought from my head. I was finished letting somebody else control my fate. That bit of courage flew out the window when something skittered across my feet. I squealed and jumped so hard my chair fell over. My shoulder and head struck hard against the ground, but I didn't think I'd broken anything.

Me: *Wait. Before you go, how did he escape with me? You and Cerberus were right there, and I saw Ronan shift as he was coming toward us.*

I'd been so sure the battle was over. I suppose it had been, but it hadn't ended the way I'd thought. We'd lost. I wanted to know how.

Lapis: *The bastard teleported with you. I'm almost positive he sedated you, then he just disappeared. Now, hold tight. We're coming for you.*

Though I hoped he was right, it made my blood boil. Here I sat, weak as ever and waiting on somebody to ride to my rescue.

A door clicked open. "Ah, you're awake. I thought for a minute I'd given you too much."

The voice was deep, and I assumed it belonged to jogger number four. Belatedly, I picked up on his last statement. I guess that explained the brain fog—they drugged me. I struggled to control my temper even through the brain fog. The last thing I needed to do was blow it up, flood it, or burn it down while I was tied to a chair.

I huffed. "Not to be cliché, but you don't know who you're dealing with. Trust me when I say it's in your own best interest to cut me loose and walk away." Considering I was lying on the floor tied to a chair, I had a feeling the threat didn't carry the weight I'd intended. Honestly, I didn't believe it myself, and despite knowing how much magic I had, I was terrified.

He chuckled, and the amusement raked my nerves. "I know exactly who I'm dealing with. A middle-aged human from the burbs who thinks she's tough shit because she found out she has a little magic. Honestly, I don't see what that shifter sees in you."

Oh boy. Not that I'd thought that would really work, but a girl could always hope. I sighed. Pointless back and forth always annoyed me in the movies. Unless it was a stall tactic, chatter was useless. If he thought that's all I was, then it would be better to let him underestimate me. Maybe I could get him to untie my hands if he thought I was that weak human who'd arrived in Florida a couple weeks before.

Instead, I muttered the truth spell and gave it a few moments to work. "What am I doing here?"

"Waiting to see the Mistress of Balance. Or at least that's her name for now."

Interesting. If the truth spell had worked, he honestly thought that's who he was working with. I debated the pros and cons of correcting him and decided nothing would be gained from making myself more valuable even if I could convince him.

"And who might that be?" I struggled to see him through the hood but couldn't make anything out other than a vague shape. The air inside the mask was thick, and sweat ran down my eyebrows and into my eyes. It had to be a hundred degrees or more in the building, and I struggled against the claustrophobia clawing at my mind.

He scoffed. "See? Just a stupid human. You have no idea what you're dabbling with. Lila Stone is going to eat you alive for wearing her necklace."

The woman's name sounded familiar, but I was struggling to figure out why.

"Where are we?" That should have been the first question I asked, but he'd thrown me off when he'd used my title for somebody else.

Boots thudded toward me across packed earth, and he wrapped his hand in my hair, using it to jerk me back upright. "That's enough with the questions."

I couldn't do much with my hands tied behind my back, and I didn't want to give away my advantage before I was in a spot to make the most of it even though I was burning to fry this guy. I opened up my mouth to say something snarky, but I never got a chance.

"Your father wasn't nearly as big a hassle as you've been." Something blunt hit my face, and for the second time that day, my world faded to black.

Chapter Twenty-Seven

"Wake up, Jules," a feminine voice said as a hand lightly slapped my face.

I struggled to open my eyes, disoriented. What I saw didn't make any sense, and when I moved my eyes, my head felt like a drum line was trying to pound its way out. I smacked my lips, peeling my tongue off the roof of my mouth.

The smells of fish and diesel fuel assaulted my nose, causing my stomach to roll. My shoulders ached when I tried to move my hands, and when I met resistance, everything came rushing back to me. I snapped my eyes open, at least as much as I could. Something sticky made it so I could only open my right eye part of the way.

I moved my head toward the voice. A tiny blonde stood directly in front of me with her hands on her hips. "I'm sorry for the rough handling. They were ordered not to hurt you, and he's been punished accordingly."

Nausea rolled over me, likely a sign I had a concussion. My vision was a little blurry around the edges as I took in the scene around me for the first time. I'd called it when I'd guessed a warehouse. Fifty-gallon drums lined the wall stacked two high, and an old flats boat perched upon a rusted trailer.

Sweat rolled down my forehead into my eyes, making it even harder to see. It stung like the dickens when it mixed with the blood.

"Gee, thanks for that," I snarked, dragging my attention back to the woman. "And just who might you be? If you didn't want me hurt, you could have just skipped the kidnapping altogether."

She lifted a shoulder. "An unfortunate necessity, I'm afraid. To answer your question, I'm Lila Stone."

As before, the name tickled the back of my mind, and I struggled through the haze to remember where I had heard it. Visions of the birth certificate I'd found in my father's safety deposit box flashed through my mind.

"Delilah Stone?" I asked.

She rolled her green eyes. "I hate that name just like you hate Juliet, but yes. My actual name is unimportant. What matters is that I'm your younger sister." Her face clouded with anger. "I didn't know about you, either. Father hid his tracks well to make sure nobody would find you. I didn't learn about you until he died and left everything to you."

The same bitterness and anger I'd felt twice before pushed against my consciousness. I'd have bet my last dollar I'd just found the source. "It was you!"

She drew her brows down in confusion. "What was me?"

Realizing I'd slipped, I shook my head. If she didn't already know about magic, I didn't want to give myself away. The fog was starting to clear from my brain, and I renewed my efforts to free my wrists.

Understanding flooded Lila's expression, and rage

joined the bitterness in her energy. She narrowed her eyes. "You're an empath just like he was!"

I stuck to my decision not to reveal my magic. I didn't know who this woman was, and if she was clueless, I wasn't giving away my advantage. "I don't know what you're talking about."

She strode toward me and pulled her arm back, then slapped me so hard my ears rang. The tequila and nacho chips I'd had at the bar pushed against the back of my throat as another wave of nausea washed over me. I resumed working on the ropes binding my wrists, doing my best to keep my shoulders still so she wouldn't catch on. Her statement worked its way into my muddled brain, freezing my hands. "I don't have a sister."

She paced in front of me, then cast me a sideways glance. "You do now, and you have for the last thirty-eight years. Well, technically, you have a half-sister. I'm not surprised he didn't tell you, though. He claimed he didn't know about me. My mother always refused to tell me who my father was, but I found a picture of them hidden in her closet when she died. She'd written his name on the back along with where it had been taken. I assume she did that so I'd be able to find him once she was gone."

It didn't make sense to me that the woman had kept her secret her entire life just to reveal it after she died. I supposed people have their reasons, but I suspected she'd kept the picture as a personal memento rather than to leave a trail of breadcrumbs for her daughter.

"How did your mom die?" I asked, then realized how insensitive the question was. Still, I wanted to know what I was dealing with, and I also needed to buy time for Ronan and Lapis to find me. She seemed like she wanted to talk, and listening to her beat getting slammed in the face by one of her minions again.

"She died in a car accident. She fell asleep driving home from her second job." Her eyes flashed with fire as her pacing became almost manic, and once again, bitterness rolled off her like dense fog. "If he'd paid child support, she wouldn't have had to work the second job. That's what fathers are supposed to do."

Ah, now we were getting to the reason behind the resentment, and it was one I could fully understand considering he'd left us too. That didn't mean I was going to run out and kidnap somebody, though, because, you know, I wasn't batshit crazy. It was a big leap to assume a random picture of her mom with Arnie was evidence he was her father. I figured that wasn't the thing to say to her right then, though. The last thing I wanted to do was bust her final rusty hinge.

"But you found him, obviously. Did he admit anything?" By this point, I was becoming invested in the story. As odd as it seemed, if she was my sister, that meant something. What, I had no idea.

She huffed out a humorless laugh, then stopped pacing and stood in front of me, nose curled in disgust. "Oh, I found him, but only because I met Drake. He made the connection and encouraged me to reach out and build a relationship. He told me if I could get close to Arnie, I'd have everything. I'd never have to go without again. People would respect me. All I had to do was get him to claim me as his heir."

This was turning into some sort of magical train wreck. I didn't want to stare, but I couldn't look away now that we were starting to put the pieces together. "Drake was your boyfriend?"

"Is," she underscored, arms crossed. "Drake *is* my fiancé. When Dad died, Drake told me I'd inherit and we could get married. Father and I had grown close, so imagine my surprise when another secret daughter turned up as the new owner of everything I'd worked for, both magical and material."

Again, that burst of rage. This time, it spiked so hard that it felt like a physical blow. Though the skin on my sweat-slick hand was raw, I felt like I was making progress. If I could just get one hand free, I'd turn the tables so fast her head would spin. Unlike Lila, I didn't plan to be a talker when my turn came.

"Don't you mean before you killed him?" I asked, remembering the comment her minion had made before he'd knocked me out.

She blinked. "Why would you say that?"

"Because that's what your guy told me before he cold-cocked me." Our father had supposedly died in a fishing accident at sea, but the man's words tumbled over and over through my head. The more I thought about it, the more sense it made.

She paused, and I could almost see the internal struggle taking place. She finally waved a hand. "Don't be ridiculous."

Even though she did her best to come across as blithe, I hoped it turned out to be something she circled back to later. Even if it wasn't the truth, sewing some seeds of discontent in the enemy camp couldn't hurt. The problem, though, is that the guy had no reason to lie. For the time being, though, I put a pin in it.

While she ranted on about Arnie, I reached out to Lapis.

Any luck finding me? Apparently, I have a sister and she's nuttier than a fruitcake.

I nearly sighed in relief when he responded immediately.

Not yet. We lost you, and without our link, I couldn't follow you.

I'd been counting on them getting closer, and to hear they weren't was a kick in the gut.

Not what I wanted to hear when I'm trying to keep a raving lunatic talking. I was unconscious. I'll keep it open, but I don't think I have much time left.

I ground my teeth in helpless frustration. With all the magic I had, I couldn't do anything without my hands. Instead, I was sitting here trussed to a chair, waiting to be rescued like some damsel in distress. I'd be remedying that hole in my training ASAP, assuming I survived this round. I tuned back into the conversation, hoping I hadn't lost the thread.

"You should be grateful, though," she continued. "Drake wants to kill you, but I think that's heavy-handed. I'd prefer to be rational, reasonable adults. Give the necklace to me. Keep the bar. You've lived your whole life without magic, so what are you really giving up?"

So she did know about magic. How much did she know about me, though? She obviously knew the necklace had power, but maybe I could gaslight her a little on the details. If I got really lucky, I might be able to kill two birds with one stone and find the ring.

"Even if I did that," I said, working my hands against the rope, "it won't do you any good. Somebody stole the ring that goes along with it, and they're a pair. The necklace won't work without it."

"Stop lying to me!" she screeched, then flew at me.

She moved so quickly I barely had time to react, but after the sucker punches I'd already taken that day, I wasn't about to absorb another. Fortunately, I didn't need my hands for that spell. I muttered the three lines the book had given me right as she drew her arm across her chest to backhand me. When her hand thwacked hard against the barrier I'd erected, I curved my lips into a satisfied grin. That probably hadn't been the smartest idea, but I was sick of being the punching bag.

She rubbed her hand, her expression venomous. "I already have the ring. We have somebody inside your little group who snatched it, and you didn't even know it was missing." She pulled a silver chain from under her floofy white blouse and held it up for me to see. The ring dangled from it, the stone winking. "Before I leave here today, I'll have the necklace too, one way or another."

Before I could absorb that, a tall, muscular, dark-haired man appeared from thin air in front of me followed shortly by five others. He moved with a grace that belied his size as he sauntered toward Lila and pulled her into a deep kiss. "I see you've done half my work for me. Why haven't you killed her yet?"

Lila pulled away from him and cast a nervous glance toward me. "I decided to try diplomacy first. I sent my men to steal the necklace from her, but it seems it's bonded with her. They couldn't get it off her neck, so they brought her to me. I'd prefer she hand it over willingly rather than find out the bond survives her death after we kill her."

He curled his lip. "No bond survives death, and we don't have the time or luxury for sentiment. Kill her."

It appeared my time was up. I put everything I had into freeing my hands. I'd almost worked one free, but it was do-or-die time, literally. I wrenched it the rest of the way from the rope, wincing as it burned through the top layer of my skin. I'd take a wicked case of rope burn over dying any day.

Electricity crackled between his hands as he turned his attention toward me. I tried to evaluate the threats as Alexa had taught me, but it was seven against one, and all of them were surely more experienced than me. I sank into an offensive stance like she'd shown me, figuring if today was my last, I was going to take at least one of them with me.

Ronan's energy burst into my consciousness right before he, Cerbi, Alexa, and Lapis burst through the doors. His gaze raked over me, then turned toward the enemy. He took two running strides, then dove into the air, leaving the ground as a man and landing as a wolf. As relieved as I was to see them all, there would be time for all that later.

Drake loosed the lightning from his palms, firing it directly at me. "No matter what," he yelled to the men standing behind him, "Don't let her get away with that necklace."

I countered with electricity of my own, and our streams met in the middle. He was powerful, but I had desperation on my side. He broke the spell and dodged my magic, changing tack. His lips moved with some spell, and I called upon the element that came easiest to me even if it was the hardest for me to control—fire.

Before Ronan could reach me, two of Drake's men attacked, one using fire while the other shifted into a bear and leapt at him, teeth and claws bared. Ronan barely had time to face them before the bear was upon him. Cerbi vaulted across the room and onto the bear's back, throwing it off balance so Ronan could get the upper hand.

Lapis half-flew, half-charged at one of the two men in the back, ripping him to shreds as Cerbi turned his attention there and dove for the other, his eyes glowing red and fangs dripping with sulphuric drool. The man shot fire at him, and Cerbi howled in pleasure as he consumed the flames then bit the man in half with his massive jaws.

The smart-ass in the back of my brain smirked. *That's what he got for going at a hellhound with his own element.*

A sleek black wolf I assumed was Alexa leapt toward Drake, and his hands twisted and turned in the air. Soil from the dirt floor of the warehouse rose and began spinning. Lightning crackled inside it as the tornado crashed toward the wolf. I blasted it with a gust of wind, and Drake roared as the funnel disintegrated into nothing more than a flurry of sand.

I spun as a high-pierced screech from my right nearly shattered my eardrums. Lila rushed toward me, her hands formed into claws as she reached for the necklace. I didn't have time to gather magic, so I did what any good Southern girl does when a mean girl is coming at her—I snatched her by her hair and used her own momentum against her.

"I owe you a black eye, *sister*," I growled, jerking her forward and down, then bringing my knees up to crash into her face. Blood spurted from her nose, and she howled. Twisting, I pulled her to the side by the hair with one hand, and let loose with the other so I could yank the chain holding the ring from around her neck.

I felt the chain break as Drake rushed forward and grabbed her arm. They both disappeared, and all fell silent.

Heart still pounding, I spun toward my friends, ring in hand. Thank the goddess, they were all still standing, apparently none the worse for the wear. I couldn't say the same for the other guys, though. Three lay dead and mangled, and a fourth sat propped against a drum, groaning. I let out a thankful sigh when I realized we'd all escaped with our lives.

Ronan, still in wolf form, trotted toward me, then nuzzled me, placing his face against mine.

I held the ring up. "I got it," I whispered, and he nudged my hand. Strands of golden light wound around us, mending it where it had broken. Ronan pushed his nose through the chain, and I slipped it over his neck. When the ring settled into the hollow of his throat, the stone pulsed with light, then went still.

His voice sounded in my head for the first time ever.

I don't ever want to experience this again. Not knowing where you were or whether you were alive or dead nearly killed me. Now we're bonded, You're mine and I'm yours. No matter what we face, we'll face it together.

I placed my hands on either side of his face and touched my forehead to his.

Forever.

Epilogue

"To Jules!" Laurel said, holding up her near-empty champagne glass.

"To Jules!" CiCi echoed.

Ronan and I raised our glasses for the toast, the sun glinting off the stone in the ring on his finger. It had been a week since we'd faced Drake and Lila and recovered it, and so far, we hadn't had any luck tracking them down. Whispers had reached us a few days later that the two were still gathering forces, so we'd doubled down on my training.

I'd learned several valuable lessons during my brief captivity, and I was focusing hard on learning to use my magic without my hands. I'd also been sparring with Ronan and Alexa, who'd decided to stick around to train me in hand-to-hand combat. It wouldn't be so easy to kidnap me a second time. Though I doubted they'd try that again, the time would come when we'd have to face them, and I wanted to be prepared.

What concerned me more than anything was Lila's claim that we had a traitor in our midst. I'd thought and thought, examining everybody in our circle, but couldn't believe any of them would betray us. Still, somebody had, and we needed to deal with it sooner rather than later. Not today, though. Today was about friends.

Laurel reached over to me and shoved my hair from my face, frowning. "That's a wicked black eye, girl. You gotta be more careful getting out of the shower, or else we're gonna hire you a full-time nurse."

That was the excuse I'd given them for the spectacular shiner I was still rocking.

CiCi, who'd already expressed her whole-hearted approval of Ronan both privately and in front of him, waggled her brows. "I'm willing to bet she's already getting the best bedside service ever. In fact, I'm willing to bet she was getting her back washed when she slipped."

My face flushed, and I grinned, not because she was right, obviously, but because we'd just enacted her scenario an hour before.

Laurel glanced around, taking in the tiki bar. They'd arrived that morning, and we'd just gotten our first drink. "This place really is great, and for what it's worth, shiner aside, it's a good look for you. I haven't seen you this happy in years."

Ronan reached under the table and squeezed my knee, winking at me.

I sighed and took a sip of my champagne. "I haven't *been* this happy in years. Maybe not ever. The boys are coming to visit for Thanksgiving break, so I'm just waiting for their stamp of approval."

"Oh, they're gonna love it as much as we do," CiCi said, waving a hand. "In fact, I'm considering packing up and moving into your guest bedroom myself."

I curved one side of my mouth into a half-smile. That would be disastrous on a number of levels, but there was no way I'd say that. I'd been a little nervous about seeing them. After all, being a bar owner in a small, Gulf Coast town was a far cry from being the wife of an Atlanta business executive. They'd embraced my new lifestyle with open arms within ten minutes of being there and had promised to visit regularly.

I drained my glass, and Ronan rose. "I'll get us another bottle. Do you ladies need anything else?"

We shook our heads, and he leaned down and gave me a toe-curling kiss.

"You gotta be shittin' me," Laurel said, her tone flat as her gaze fixed on something behind me.

Ronan straightened, and I froze when I heard a voice that now sounded like nails on a chalkboard to me.

"Nice to see you settling into your little fantasy life already," Rob said, his tone a mixture of condescension and disgust. "Obviously, the day drinking has lowered your standards."

My back stiffened, and Ronan growled low in his throat. If he'd been in wolf form, his hackles would have gone up.

He turned quickly, his movements smooth and lethal. "You must be the man who was foolish enough to let Jules go. I suppose I should thank you because it worked out well for me. Rest assured, I won't make the same mistake. I don't think Jules has any complaints, either."

Just the sound of Rob's voice had sent my blood pressure through the roof, but watching Ronan take him down without missing a beat sent a petty little thrill through me. The best part was that I sensed the absolute honesty in his statement.

Rob bristled, but it wasn't like he had much room to say anything. Instead, he stepped around Ronan and glared at me. "This nonsense has gone on long enough. You need to come home so we can sort this out."

I furrowed my brow, confused. "What's there to sort out? CiCi and Laurel were kind enough to stop by the house to pick up my picture albums and some other things from the boys' childhoods before they came. There's officially nothing left for me to sort other than signing the divorce papers, and I can do that from here."

Ronan remained standing and placed his hand on my shoulder.

Rob's gaze slid to his hand. "There aren't going to be any divorce papers if I can help it, Jules. I made a terrible mistake. Let's go home and work this out."

I blinked a couple times, unable to believe what had just come out of his mouth, "You made a mistake? A *mistake?*" My tone rose an octave, but Ronan squeezed my shoulder before I had a chance to blow anything up. Honestly, though, I was more pissed at Rob's gall than I was hurt.

CiCi snickered. "What happened, Rob? Did Bubbles leave you for a younger buck when she realized you weren't the cash cow she thought you were?"

Laurel held up a hand. "No need to answer. We already heard she and Scott Levine have been sporting around town in her new Porsche."

My jaw fell open. Scott Levine was an up-and-coming junior partner at the most prestigious law firm in Atlanta. He was young, hot, and on his way up the ladder.

"Sorry, Jules," CiCi said under her breath. "We were saving that one for the next toast."

I laughed, and suddenly, what Rob did or did not do made no difference to me. I didn't wish him ill, but there was no place in my world for him anymore. I'd given him twenty years of my life. I didn't regret that, if for no other reason than I'd gotten two beautiful boys from it, but now it was time to turn the page and start the next chapter of my life.

I smiled, content, and watched my past walk out the door as my future took my hand.

* * *

Join Jules and Ronan as they continue their journey in Book 2, Hair of the Demon Dog.

A Note from Tegan

This book has been an adventure for me, and I've enjoyed both stepping outside the cozy genre and writing about an older main character. It was nice to work with somebody who has those aches and pains and emotional depth that come from experience, and I hope you enjoyed visiting Dolphin Key as much as I did!

The next book in the series, Hair of the Demon Dog, will be just as much fun as Jules, Ronan, and crew navigate the next leg of their journey to balance good and evil while finding love and drinking fruity cocktails on the beach! I hope you decide to join us again.

If you'd like to keep track of new releases, you can do that by
    Joining my newsletter
    Joining The Cracked Cauldron Facebook Group
    Following me on Amazon

Acknowledgments

This book wouldn't be complete if I didn't mention my sister's impact on my writing career and this book in particular. Since way back when I first started writing Sweet Murder, my first book, she's been there. She's helped me with everything from spitballing ideas to critiquing covers (you wouldn't even believe some of the ways we've come up with to kill people!). Most importantly, she's always been there for me through the personal stuff - wins and losses, ups and downs.

With Champagne Witches, I was coming back from a really dark place while recovering from some serious health issues. She helped me find my bootstraps and took my elbow to help me pull myself back up. We plotted this book together, and there's a lot of her in it. She was, as always, a true sister, and this book wouldn't exist in its current form without her.

Also by Tegan Maher

Witches of Keyhole Lake

Enchanted Coast Magical Mysteries

Paranormal Artifacts

Cori Sloane Witch Mysteries

Witches of Abaddon's Gate

Haunted Lodge Cozy Mysteries

Gulf Coast Reaper Series (Coming Soon!)

Printed in Great Britain
by Amazon

86999947R00137